The Red Speck

•

S. Conde

The Red Speck

Idols of the Tribe

© 2012 by S. Conde

Cover design by Dylan Vigil at VehemenceDesign.com.

Printed in the United States of America

Table of Contents

This book is dedicated to those who have known

pain, struggle, and sacrifice,

yet still marvel at the overwhelming beauty of life.

Chapter One : Commencement

The beautiful man drove a 1979 maroon and white Oldsmobile down Biscayne Boulevard in North Miami Beach. He sped along with the windows open allowing the cool ocean breeze to blow in freely, tousling his dark, wavy hair. "Fly Like an Eagle" was playing on the radio.

"Time keeps on slippin', slippin', slippin' into the future..."

It was nearing dusk that day in late September, and the salty evening air was less oppressive than usual, crisp even. The man turned off the radio, with a loud click. The melody was far too pleasant to suit his mood. He was angry, very angry. In fact, he was shouting.

"You bitch! Why are you trying to ruin my life?! I am NOT getting another divorce!"

The powerful man shook his head no for emphasis. He seemed very committed to his last statement. She listened and watched him from the passenger seat, silently awaiting what would come next. ...afraid to speak.

He had been divorced twice already and viewed the ending of those relationships as personal failures, although he would never openly admit such a thing, not even to himself. No, it was very important to him that everyone knew he was blameless. His ex wives were crazy, manipulative liars and adulteresses. Which may have actually been true, still, she often wondered why he chose the same types over and over.

"You fucking cunt! I will NOT let you do this to me!", the charming man continued.

It was as though she'd been punched in the stomach. That was a word she'd never heard him use before, and now he was using it to describe her. She felt physically ill.

This was not how she imagined the ride would go. She was quite happy to get in the car, excited to finally have a chance to be alone with him so she could explain herself, so she could tell him the truth about what had been happening while he was away.

It seemed they were never alone anymore. They used to climb into the abandoned lifeguard stands at Haulover Beach long after the sunbathers and tourists had gone home. They would sit up there, sheltered from the wind and talk for hours. She missed those days terribly, even now. The truth is that she loved him. He was her first true love. No matter what he said, no matter what he did, she would always love him in a way that she would never love anyone else.

He continued to shout at her. Her response was to cry. Unfortunately, her tears only served to anger him further.

He turned east toward the beach, then left onto a dirt road which eventually opened up into a clearing. Just beyond the clearing was a dense patch of Mother Nature, thick wooded and wild. He hadn't answered earlier when she asked where they were going.

Her sobbing slowed as she became increasingly aware of their surroundings. She was confused. The angry man slammed his foot down hard on the brakes. A sea of white dust rose up from behind the car, slowly engulfing the vehicle. He reached across his passenger and flung open her door.

"Get out!"

"Wh-what?", was all she could muster.

"Get the fuck out!", came his response. She jumped back as though she'd been slapped. He just glared at her. His eyes were dark and cloudy, completely devoid of compassion. She searched, but didn't recognize a shred of the man she loved in those eyes.

As always, she did what he asked of her. She got out. He pulled the door closed, threw the car in reverse and spun the 1979 maroon and white Oldsmobile around. The violent action caused a million and one tiny bits of crushed rock and seashell to fly up in her face. She instinctively held her hands up in front of her eyes. He hit the gas and made his escape. She was no longer his concern, discarded in the woods like a dog who had chewed her last shoe.

There she stood in the white dust, pelted by it, covered with it. She cried out,

"Daddy, come back!" The little girl screamed those words over and over again. It was pointless, pathetic even. He wasn't listening. He had stopped listening a long time ago.

She watched through the haze of dust and tears as the tail lights of the car grew smaller and smaller in the distance until they merged into nothing more than one tiny red speck. The red speck eventually disappeared into the night.

The ten year old girl was terrified. She often watched the news with her grandparents and knew very well what could happen to a girl alone at night in a deserted area. Her heart felt as though it would beat right through her chest. She peered wildly around in all directions.

"Calm down!", she shouted impatiently at herself. Slowly she regained her composure. Her heart still beat uncontrollably fast, but she managed to shift her mind from despair into survival mode. She had no idea how to get home, but she remembered the last two turns they had made to get here and that, at least, was a start. Maybe she'd find a pay phone along the way. She would call her grandmother collect. She could always count on her grandmother, maybe she'd move in with her again. She hoped so.

Her plan in place, the girl began walking in the direction of the red speck. As she took the first steps on her journey home, headlights turned onto the dirt road that led to the clearing. She froze in her tracks and tried desperately to make out details of the car. Though as yet undiagnosed, the girl's vision was horrible. Maybe her father had come back for her, or maybe it was one of those bad men she'd seen on the news that rape and murder little girls and leave their dead bodies in ditches on the side of the road.

While the girl was distracted by the unfolding of events, a storm had begun rolling in from offshore. As she stood there, helplessly trying to discern any distinguishing characteristics of the car, the entire sky above her seemed to split open with a loud crack and rain down huge droplets of cold water, further obscuring her view.

She reasoned with herself that it must be her father. What were the odds of another car turning down the same dirt road to nowhere in such a short period of time? ...and at night, in this weather? She was unsure, and stuck in the mud between the car and the woods. As she stood there freezing, heart racing, she remembered something she once heard about choosing between the devil you know and the devil you don't. In the time it took the next flash of lightning to illuminate the sky, she chose her devil. The girl ran toward the woods. She ran from the lightning, from the rain, and from the bad men, but mostly, she ran from her father.

The car continued toward her, but the girl was fast, very fast, the fastest of all the girls *and* boys in her class. Her long, thin body flew over the white mud and leapt over quickly forming puddles. She hadn't counted on how slippery the vegetation would be when she made the transition from mud to leaves, and didn't adjust her gait. She slid forward and hit her head on a fallen branch. It hurt, but she knew the car was still very close. She got up and took off running again. She ran for what seemed like forever. The girl was deep in the woods when she finally slowed to a walk. The rain was still coming down hard. She knew she'd been bleeding for some time as she tasted the blood mixed with rainwater that ran from her forehead to her lips and beyond.

A few feet in front of her was a huge banyan tree. Some of its roots were as tall as she was. The girl carefully nestled herself into a spot between two enormous roots, leaning her back against one of them. She sat, panting, in the shelter of the banyan, mentally, physically and emotionally exhausted. She was protected from the rain by the massive canopy of the tree. She was safe at last. The young girl closed her eyes and imagined herself as part of the ancient banyan. Roots sprouted from the soles of her feet; they reached deep into the earth. The soil warmed her. She was comforted by the vibrations of the natural world rising up through her feet. She was filled with a sense of calm. She smelled the ocean air and felt the breeze flow gently through her hair just as it moved through the leaves of the mighty tree. The girl felt strong and proud of herself for coming this far on her own, she was responsible for her survival. She could take care of herself. She wondered for a moment if she would ever find her way home. Then she wondered if that was what she really wanted.

Just as she drifted off to sleep she felt a strange sensation, as if she were floating. She heard a woman's voice speaking softly in a foreign language, Spanish maybe. The girl could smell the woman's breath, it was sweet, like honey.

Chapter Two : Failure to Grasp

Sophie was a beautiful woman, tall and thin with light, almost clear, blue green eyes and long dark wavy hair. She had a warm smile and a kind heart. Her smile and the twinkle in her eyes, though genuine, veiled a long standing suffering within, but her veil was thick and only those who took the time to truly regard her rather than simply look at her, could see beyond the veil. Sophie, when questioned, was dismissive, believing she had no right to complain when others had suffered so much more. After all, she would say, she was never raped, nor beaten. As far as most people could tell, she was a very together young woman, with a "good head on her shoulders". Which was just how she liked it. She was horrified when someone witnessed the tangled mess of disturbing emotions, insecurity, and pain lurking just below the surface. She was too young, or perhaps too naive, to realize that she had a lot in common with those who could easily see her for who she really was.

She was twenty four years old and currently, completely disoriented. Sophie awoke to find herself on a crescent shaped stretch of deserted beach sometime well after noon. The place was vaguely familiar, and she was dressed appropriately, in a peach colored bikini, but she had no idea how she'd arrived.

Her head throbbed. Had she been drinking? she wondered. She didn't think so. She looked around carefully for a clue, and found nothing. There were no footprints nor impressions in the sand around her at all. It was as though she simply appeared.

Sophie could feel the anxiety begin in the pit of her stomach and radiate upward and outward, overtaking her normal breathing pattern. In a matter of seconds her heart was beating aggressively. She knew, from past experience, that she was not having a heart attack, just another panic attack. She closed her eyes and tried to breathe through it. She knew if she could get her breathing under control, her heart would follow. She focused all her energy on her breathing. Counting to four on the inhale, holding for the count of eight, and exhaling to the count of twelve. Slowly the ancient method began to work and the panic attack subsided. When she opened her eyes she was still alone on the pristine shore and still clueless as to where she was and how she had arrived there, but at least she was calm.

She stood up, dusted the sand off her youthful backside and had a look around. Behind her was a forested area, in front of her was the ocean and to either side was a beautiful stretch of abandoned golden sand. Sophie stared out at the ocean, it was definitely the Atlantic. She grew up in and around the Atlantic Ocean. She knew its smell, color, and sound. It called to her. The ocean had always been a strong force in her life. She had made most of her biggest decisions either sitting on its shoreline or completely submerged in its waters. Sophie considered the ocean a friend, a confidant, feminine and often fierce. She recognized something of herself in its patterns. More than anything, the ocean was the one place where Sophie was able to completely relax. Though her life was full of inconsistencies, the ocean was always there for her. Predictable in its unpredictability.

Sophie walked out into the calm and shallow water. It was warm...soothing. She strode out further until she was waist deep then dove under. When she popped back up a few yards away her hair was slicked back. The water had the effect of a tranquilizer on her. She breathed in deeply and exhaled, "Much better.", she said out loud.

She rolled over in the water as she had done a million times before, and began to float. Her grandfather taught her how to float and tread water as life saving techniques when she was a child. Sophie had embraced floating completely. Laying on top of the water and undulating with the flow of the tide, rather than fighting against it, was so incredibly peaceful. Floating, she thought, is all about breath control and doing nothing. As soon as you actively try to float, your muscles tense up and you sink.

As she lay there on top of the water, bobbing up and down with the waves, pondering the nothingness of floating and feeling the familiar warmth of the sun on her skin, she suddenly became aware of another presence in the water. She felt it with every fiber of her being; she was definitely not alone. Sophie opened her eyes and pushed her body underwater, she whipped her head around and saw a woman floating calmly next to her. She was striking, caramel colored, curvier and slightly shorter than Sophie. Her hair was long and black. A few strands had seashells braided into them. While her hair partially obscured her breasts Sophie could easily see that she was both topless and in perfect proportion to her hips. Sophie imagined her to be about thirty.

The woman did not react to Sophie's splashes nor the waves she had made. In fact the water around the woman was not altered at all by the motion and remained oddly calm, as though her own waves of energy canceled out the waves Sophie had created. She floated in her own personal ocean, completely undisturbed by the ripples caused by others.

The woman turned her head toward Sophie, and with her eyes still closed asked,

"Where have you been?"

Sophie detected a slight accent, Cuban she thought. She was even more confused than before, and rapidly treading water.

"Excuse me, what? Have we met?"

The woman opened her exquisite black almond shaped eyes and smiled. Sophie was starting to feel the anxiety creep back, the woman noticed. She slowly turned her face back toward the sun and closed her eyes.

"I mean you no harm. Please, go back to floating. It's so peaceful don't you think?"

This was weird. Beyond weird. Nevertheless, she allowed her body to float back up, and in doing so was forced to relax. Anyway she thought, maybe she can tell me where I am.

"Yes", said Sophie, "it is. I was just thinking the same thing."

They floated in silence for several minutes. "Do you know me?" Sophie asked.

The woman smiled, eyes closed, "I do."

"Do I know you?" The minute the words left her lips she deemed them ridiculous, but it was too late.

"Yes, you do." came the woman's reply.

Not so ridiculous after all.

Sophie considered amnesia, but dismissed the thought immediately. After all she knew *who* she was, just not *where* she was...how she got here...nor who the semi nude woman, who had apparently been expecting her, was.

Sophie's mind wrestled with the bizarre reality of her situation. No matter how her mind twisted and turned the facts around in her head, they still made no sense at all. Neither Sophie nor her mind were accustomed to highly improbable circumstances such as these. Rationality, cause and effect, these were the contexts Sophie understood.

As Sophie was about to postulate her next question, the woman opened her eyes. "We're here!", she exclaimed happily.

Sophie, still unsure where "there" was, opened her eyes to see where "here" was and was nearly blinded.

"Oh my God!", Sophie exclaimed shielding her eyes with her hands.

"I know, it's bright in the daylight. It's really meant to be seen at night, by the light of the moon."

"Where are we?" asked Sophie.

"My house." came the response.

As Sophie slowly blinked her eyes open the woman was already halfway up the ladder.

"Come up!" said the smiling woman.

This time Sophie knew not to look directly at the beautiful stilt house which was completely covered in what appeared to be mother of pearl shingles. She swam over to the ladder and climbed up onto the wraparound porch.

"Let me get you a towel" said the woman as she skipped off into the house.

Sophie paused for a moment to take in her surroundings. "How did I not see this from the shore? It's like a beacon of blinding white light for God's sake", she thought to herself. She had passed stilt houses a million times, they fascinated her, but she had never actually been in one, and none of the ones she saw looked like this. They were usually little more than shanty's on sticks. This house however, was incredible. The floor, at least that of the porch, was made of wide coral tiles. "Illegal", Sophie thought. She had grown up amongst houses covered in sheets of coral. Though she understood why it was now illegal to tear apart living coral reefs for building materials, and was in complete agreement with the new ruling, she did miss seeing coral slabs commonly. They were so beautiful, and a precious fond memory of her youth.

On the porch was a gorgeous swing hanging from the ceiling. It was layered in what appeared to be hammered silver. "It looks Indonesian", she thought. The bench itself was upholstered in aquamarine silk with matching pillows arranged carefully on top. How the woman managed to maintain the swing in such salty air was beyond her. As she stood there considering the upkeep of such a home, the woman returned. She was wearing a beautifully flowing, blue gauze dress with white trim and carrying a fluffy white towel for Sophie.

"Thank you." she said as she took the towel and dried off.

The woman smiled again, "Come in, come in."

Sophie obliged. The inside of the house was less spectacular than the outside, but warm and comfortable, with a distinctly oceanic theme. The interior walls were lined with woven sea grass, as was the floor, the paddles of the ceiling fans were made from purple sea fans, and the dining room table was comprised of a twisted silver colored driftwood base, topped with a very large irregularly shaped piece of bluish green sea glass. Sophie had found sea glass along the shoreline many times before, in fact she used to collect pieces when she was a little girl and save them in a box with her most treasured possessions. Sophie walked over to the table and ran her hand across the surface. "This is incredible! Did you find it yourself?", she asked.

"Yes, while I was swimming.", said Maria.

"Wow.", Sophie said as she knelt down to look at the underside of the table.

Because sea glass is made semi opaque and smooth by the ocean, turned over and over in the waves and rubbed non stop with millions of grains of sand, finding a piece the size of your hand is exceedingly rare. Seeing a piece this size...Sophie was entranced.

"How did you get it up here?"

The woman laughed, enjoying Sophie's fascination with the table top. "You'd be surprised what you can do when you put your mind to it."

Sophie stood up and turned to the woman while still touching the glass. "What do you think it was? ...a window?"

The woman put her left hand on the table and closed her eyes. She tilted her head to the right as if she were listening for something. "It was part of a glass shower enclosure from a yacht that sank not too far from here." The woman opened her eyes and lifted her hand from the table. Sophie instantly knew the woman was right. Apart from the size and shape, glass records sound...

The woman's eyes narrowed as she looked at Sophie.

"You heard it too."

Sophie shrugged her shoulders. I'm not sure what I heard. ...probably just the ocean outside."

The woman laughed. "Yes, that would be most probable."

"Let me show you to the guest room.", she said changing the subject. "I laid out something for you to wear on the bed."

"Guest room?", said Sophie. "Oh no, I'm not staying...I mean thank you, but I couldn't. I don't even know where I am. I've got to get home."

The woman smiled a kind and understanding smile. "No te preocupes...don't worry. I'm here to help you. If you don't want to stay that's fine, but at least go change into something more comfortable while I make dinner. You must be starving. We can talk over dinner."

The woman made sense, and she was remarkably hungry. Anyway, thought Sophie, what am I going to do? Swim back to shore at sunset? ...to go where? "Ok", she said. "Thank you."

The woman looked up and smiled. "Good. Oh, and if you want to rinse off there's a fresh water shower outside on the deck...you'll figure it out."

Without instruction, Sophie walked past a huge pile of comfy looking blue and white throw pillows that covered the floor in a corner of the room which was sectioned off by white mosquito netting. She moved down the hall, opened the first door on her left and went inside. Not surprisingly, the room was lovely. The heavy four post bed was made of a very deep brown wood Sophie didn't recognize, and carved in an old Spanish style. Its canopy was made of the most delicate dark blue fabric, with tiny crystals sewn all over the underside. The crystals mimicked the layout of the constellations.

The bed linens where white and soft to the touch. Past the bed were two teak slatted doors, which opened to reveal the fresh water shower. The shower was surrounded by a shoulder high semi circle of ornate teak lattice, inlaid with mother of pearl. On either side of the shower were huge jade planters filled with night blooming jasmine, and above the shower was nothing but blue sky. I could not have imagined a more beautiful place, Sophie thought to herself.

She hung the towel on the hook provided, removed her bathing suit and let the water flow. As she rinsed the salt from her hair and body she wondered what the woman meant. She said she was here to help her. How? ...and how did she know her? Sophie was certain the woman heard the same thing she did when she listened to the table. Beyond the newly recorded sound of the tides was the distinct sound of water being sprayed from a shower head. I wonder if she heard the singing too, Sophie wondered. Sophie felt the familiar pang just under her belly button, accompanied by a quick tightening of the solar plexus, a feeling of shame and a sudden burst of irrational fear. What is wrong with me?, she wondered as she turned off the water.

Sitting in a nook of the shower was a cobalt blue bottle with a silver dropper. Sophie opened it and smelled the most wonderfully fragrant lavender oil. She squeezed a few drops into the palm of her hand and rubbed it all over her wet body. I hope she doesn't mind, worried Sophie unnecessarily. She dried off and dressed herself in the delicate white cotton dress the woman had chosen for her. On the dresser was an antique tortoise shell comb. Sophie stood in front of the mirror and looked at herself as she combed her long bronze tipped mahogany hair. She found the sadness in her eyes repellant, and tuned her gaze away. She had been unable to look at herself with compassion for years.

Chapter Three : Cognitive Dissonance

The two women sat at opposite ends of the driftwood table. The flickering candlelight caressed them both in a soft warm glow. The table was set with silver, linen, china and a white coral vase filled with Irises. It was elegant but very comfortable and relaxed, not stuffy at all. They began the meal with oysters on the half shell. Oysters wouldn't have been Sophie's first choice, but these were remarkable. They were the freshest she had ever tasted.

"These are amazing.", Sophie said as she squeezed half a lemon over the oyster on her plate.

"Thank you", said the woman. "There's an oyster bed under the house."

Interesting, thought Sophie. She wondered how many people could say that.

"I'm embarrassed to mention this, but I don't even know your name", said Sophie.

The woman smiled, "There's no need to be embarrassed, I go by a lot of names actually."

"Well then," smiled Sophie, "...which do you prefer to use in causal conversation?"

Having known many actresses and other questionable figures of dubious origin,

Sophie naturally assumed the woman was either referring to a stage name, or a name she used in her native country before moving here.

The woman laughed. "You can call me Maria."

Sophie returned the smile, "Maria, pleased to meet you. I'm..."

"Sophie." Maria finished her sentence.

"How do you know my name?", Sophie demanded.

"How does a mother not know her daughter?"

"What? I mean...pardon me?"

"Perhaps we should finish dinner first, then..."

"No!" interrupted Sophie. She was instantly ashamed by her impatient outburst. The woman had been nothing but kind to her. Maria tilted her head and regarded Sophie with a bemused expression.

"Maria, I'm sorry. Please know that I'm so grateful for your hospitality and I don't mean to be rude, but I need to know what's going on. I don't know where I am, nor how I got here...I have a headache that won't go away..." Sophie rubbed her head as she started to feel the room spin. She tried hard to focus her eyes on the table in front of her, but the harder she tried to focus the less clearly she was able to see. This time was different than the others, she felt a strange tugging sensation near her belly button as though someone was trying to pull her away by a phantom umbilical cord tethered to her body.

Maria arose from her seat and rushed to her aid. "Breathe", instructed Maria, "...in through the nose out through the mouth. Just relax, close your eyes and breathe."

Sophie did what Maria told her to do.

"Don't try to grasp any of this...", Maria said gesturing to herself and the house, "...just listen to my voice and breathe, stay here with me." As her breathing started to return to normal, Sophie slowly opened her eyes.

"Be careful," Maria said, "not to focus your eyes too well on anything, keep your gaze soft for now."

Maria held a water glass to Sophie's lips.

"Drink a little of this."

"What is it?"

"An omiero...sort of a sacred...drink..." Maria said, not wanting to get into a long explanation of the details involved in making a specific omiero, nor its uses. "I made it for you earlier, it won't hurt you."

Sophie sipped the strange tasting liquid tentatively.

"Feeling better?" asked Maria.

Sophie nodded her head.

"Come with me." Maria helped Sophie up from the table and guided her over to the corner of the room that was strewn with a mass of blue and white embroidered pillows. She parted the mosquito net with her hand.

"Here, lie down." Maria arranged the pillows for Sophie and helped ease her down to the floor. Maria sat next to her.

"Sophie...", she began, "...this, mi hija, is part of the reason you are here. We need to work on...this.", she said as she gestured to Sophie's prostrate body on the floor. "As soon as you start to get close to the truth, you panic."

Sophie looked puzzled and still a little pale, as though her grasp on this world was tenuous at best.

"Listen to me." Maria continued. "I will tell you a story." Maria pulled her legs in toward her body, and sat cross legged on the floor. "A very long time ago the world was nothing...darkness, a void. Then one day the creator had a thought. ...a thought of what should be. The thought became a vision, a clear picture of the world to come. Once the vision was perfectly formed, the creator spoke of the vision out loud. The words had such powerful vibrations that they shook the void, causing tiny particles of nothingness to shake loose. The creator's airy heart was warmed by what had been accomplished, which fed the fire of the creator's will. The creator moulded the particles together tightly with mighty hands and made them molten with the fire of will. The waters of life were added to the world, they cooled the hot mass which solidified the thought and created earth."

Sophie listened to Maria's tale with genuine interest, but had no idea how any of this pertained to her, where the hell she was, nor how she was going to get home.

Maria laughed seeming to read her thoughts. "Mind over matter, Sophie. Thoughts create reality. ...I wouldn't wish your thoughts on my worst enemy. What sort of reality have you built for yourself based on your thoughts?"

Sophie considered Maria's question. What sort of reality had she built herself? ...an unpleasant one, she thought.

Both her thoughts and her life were complicated. She was naturally a happy person who was able to find joy in the simplest of pleasures, beauty in the most common of things. Lately though she had twice caught herself contemplating driving her car off the Julia Tuttle Causeway. If she were a more selfish person, she might have. Instead she thought about those who would be left wondering why they weren't important enough reasons for her to go on living. Her train of thought stopped abruptly as a very different thought crossed the tracks.

"How do you know my thoughts?"

Maria brought her hand to her forehead in a gesture of exasperation. "Why do you focus on the minutia?"

"I wasn't aware that mind reading was minutia. That seems like a pretty big deal to me."

"Fine, maybe so, and we'll get there. For now let's say I'm not reading your mind...I just know you very well. Now, to the more important question...are you happy with the life that you are living?"

"No.", Sophie replied unequivocally, "I am not. I am not living the life I had hoped for when I was a little girl."

Maria nodded her head knowingly. "Think about my story Sophie. You need to work it in reverse on a personal level." Maria paused. "I can't tell you exactly where you are...", said Maria, "...but I can say that it's easier to leave here than it is to return. I can also tell you that you are here because you want to be here, you actively sought this place out. So, if I were you, I'd stop worrying so much about getting home and more about what home actually means."

****

That night Sophie didn't sleep. She lay in the bed, under the canopy of crystal constellations having accepted Maria's invitation to stay indefinitely. She would simply accept that she appeared on the beach from out of nowhere. The simple decision freed her considerably. She was happy to be relieved of the heavy burdens, of "why" and "how" she had been carrying since she arrived. *I am not going to drive myself crazy trying to figure this out. I am here, and that's all I need to know for now. It is what it is,* she thought.

Sophie was still feeling the effects of the drink Maria had given her. At the time she was too dizzy to explain to Maria that she knew exactly what an omiero was, and how sipping it was a supreme act of trust, since an omiero can be made to achieve any number of purposes. Sophie couldn't remember exactly how she knew this, but it seemed someone very close to her once explained that an omiero is simply a potion, and as such, can be made of nearly anything. Judging by how pleasantly relaxed Sophie felt, Maria's intentions were clearly positive.

She lay there as the ocean breeze drifted in through the open door to the shower, carrying with it the fragrance of jasmine. She could see the stars clearly from the bed. Sophie didn't remember ever seeing them shine so brightly. The canopy billowed with the draft of cool night air. As she practiced letting go, the tiny quartz crystals moved across the dark blue fabric and formed the signs of the zodiac. She paid particular attention to the scorpion, as it was her sign. The stinger on its tail bounced almost imperceptibly as it crawled toward the center of the canopy. She continued to passively look upon her sign while the other symbols migrated toward the scorpion. One by one they merged with the scorpion, who grew in size with each new addition. Ultimately, only the centaur remained distinct from the magnetic creature. The two signs appeared to be locked in a duel. The scorpion faced the centaur with its stinger raised high, while the centaur faced the scorpion with its arrow drawn. Before the giant scorpion could attack, the archer let his arrow fly, piercing the scorpion in the heart. Sophie flinched. The arrow didn't kill the scorpion but instead produced a transformation. The crystals that had comprised the scorpion again rearranged themselves into the form of an eagle. Sophie was pleased. The centaur galloped over to the massive eagle willingly, allowing the eagle to wrap its talons carefully around the

24

centaurs body. Sophie watched in amazement as the eagle flew with the centaur held gently in its grasp off the canopy out the door and into the sky. It didn't take long before Sophie lost sight of the crystal creatures against the backdrop of the stars.

Sophie returned her attention to the canopy only to find the crystals in their original constellations. She watched them carefully for a while to see if they would move again, but they didn't. Eventually she closed her eyes and allowed her mind to drift naturally from thought to thought. Images of Maria, the beautiful and blinding white house, the crystal creatures and the ocean waves danced in her head. She thought of Maria's story of creation. Work it backwards she had said. Earth, to water, to fire, to air, to sound to thought? It seemed something was missing. Sophie didn't understand, still she allowed her mind to play gently with images of each concept. Before long the sun rose, gradually filling the room with soft light. She was excited to see what the new day would bring.

Chapter Four : Affinity

Sophie made her way to the kitchen where she found Maria already at work.

"Good morning!", sang Maria. "I've made you tea, it's agrimony...kind of an acquired taste, but with enough honey anything is good!" Maria smiled and handed Sophie a cup. "...except wormwood...", Maria mumbled as she began preparing a fruit salad by slicing the carambola, "...nothing helps the taste of that...horrible." Maria shuddered.

"Thank you." said Sophie, suddenly relieved she hadn't been handed a cup of wormwood, whatever that was. The tea tasted a bit odd but not terrible.

"More honey?", asked Maria.

"No...", laughed Sophie, "...it's fine."

"How did you sleep?", Maria asked.

Not wanting to hurt Maria's feelings Sophie kept her sleeplessness to herself. She felt well rested though, and that, she decided to share.

"I am completely refreshed," Sophie replied, rather pleased with herself.

Maria looked at her sideways.

"The agrimony will help with that.", Maria replied as she began cutting a mango into cubes.

"With what?"

"Authenticity."

Sophie was taken aback. "I was being honest."

"Honest yes, authentic no." Maria remarked.

"Seriously?", said Sophie, with more than a small hint of sarcasm.

"Seriously.", replied Maria as she slid her hand down the cutting board dropping the mango into a large white bowl with the waiting star fruit. She pulled a banana from the bunch sitting on the white stone counter and went to work.

"Fine." Sophie sighed loudly for effect and went on, "I didn't sleep at all, but somehow I feel remarkably rested, revived even. I just didn't want to make you feel badly by telling you I didn't sleep. Also, while I'm at it, are you aware that the crystals on your canopy have a life of their own?"

Maria smiled broadly. "That's more like it. ...and yes, I am." She continued, "Why do you worry so much about other people's feelings?"

Sophie thought that a very odd question. Worrying about every detail of what she did and said in terms of how it would effect others was part of her programming. It was part of what being a good person was all about, Sophie thought.

"It must be exhausting constantly trying to guess how your words are going to make someone else feel. I'm not saying you should be purposely hurtful, in fact you should avoid being hurtful, but come on your truth is your truth, everyone is responsible for their own feelings."

Sophie wondered if that were true. When *did* she become responsible for the world's feelings? Both Maria and Sophie knew that it was more than just not wanting to hurt people's feelings, there was a deep seated fear there, of being misunderstood...of retribution.

"It *is* exhausting!", Sophie laughed. "...and I'm good at it. I mean, it's easy to guess what people want to hear. I don't lie to them, but I do try to make the truth more..." Sophie turned her eyes upward, as though the word she was looking for might drop from the sky, and then it did. "...pleasant."

"Well, that's understandable, not wanting to hurt people...", said Maria.

"No one, but me apparently, really wants to hear the truth. They say they want to know how you feel...but then when you actually tell them it's all tears and anger."

Maria smiled at Sophie and served her a small bowl of the fruit salad.

"Not always.", she said.

"In my experience, nearly always." Sophie picked up the fork Maria had set down for her and took a bite of the mango. It was perfectly ripe and sweet. Sophie smiled appreciatively.

"I'm glad you like it", said Maria, "I think you need some new experiences."

Sophie covered her mouth to keep the mango from shooting out as she laughed, "Me too!"

****

Sophie stood at the sink washing up after breakfast. She felt so comfortable here. More comfortable than she felt around her own family, but then that wasn't much of a surprise, she thought. Almost every close relationship in her life incorporated the themes of abandonment and betrayal. She hadn't realized that fact until this very moment.

She turned to wipe down the counter when Maria floated into the room.

Sophie smiled, "You look beautiful, like a goddess!"

Maria winked at her and spun around to provide Sophie with a better view. The smell of coconut oil wafted past Sophie on the subtle breeze Maria had created. She wore a long white gauzy dress, which lifted up and out slightly as she turned. Her black hair flowed down her back, thick sections of her tresses wrapped loosely in tiny strands of pearls.

Maria stopped spinning, the bottom of her dress continued for another half turn then came to rest at her ankles.

"I have to go take care of some business today, then I'm going to my sisters afterward for a party. „,of course you're invited."

Sophie smiled, "Thank you."

Maria nodded. "I left something for you to wear on the bed, I hope you like it."

"I'm sure I'll love it."

Maria turned to leave, then stopped short, "Oh, I almost forgot. A dear friend is coming over later this morning. I told him you were here. He'll get you to the party. ...that is of course if you decide to go."

"Why wouldn't I go?"

Maria paused, "Who knows what could happen between now and then?"

"Hmmm.", Sophie raised her left eyebrow as she was prone to do, in response.

"Well if I do decide to go, what time...", Sophie started then realized she had no watch and hadn't seen a clock since she arrived.

Maria waved her hand dismissively in the air as she headed out the door. "Time doesn't matter. Come when you're ready, if you're ready...if you want. Just do whatever feels natural." Sophie smiled as she watched Maria leave, she liked her more and more by the minute.

Sophie remained at the counter, smiling, waiting for something she didn't know she was waiting for, until it didn't arrive. Where was the noise? Strange, she thought and moved over to the doorway then out onto the porch. Nothing. No boat motor, no oars, no splash. Sophie looked down into the clear blue water. There were oysters, tons of them actually, and plenty of brightly colored fish, but no Maria. Sophie started to stress for a minute then thought...why? ...to what end? Maria was rubbing off.

She turned to go back inside and glanced at the swing, it was irresistible. She spread out on the floating bench, resting her head on the pillows and dangling her feet off the side. The day was perfect, the sky was clear blue and the sound of the waves lapping gently against the stilts of the house was rhythmic and soothing. Sophie closed her eyes and let her mind wander again. ...a dear friend... She wondered who was coming for her. No matter, Maria said he'd come and that was enough. Sophie was glad she decided to stay.

The breeze blowing in over the waves kept the heat of the sun in check. She lost track of time as she relaxed into herself on the swing. Sophie loved a porch swing. It reminded her of her grandmother, the one constant positive force in her life. She and her meemaw would sip iced tea and sit on the porch swing for hours. They talked about everything and nothing. Sometimes they would just swing in silence, listening to the crickets and enjoying the comfort of each others company. The more she thought of her grandmother the more peaceful she felt. She could feel the love growing inside of her and flowing out from her chest and back, as though her heart simply wasn't big enough to contain all the love she felt for the old woman.

As she lay there, basking in the glory of love, she heard what sounded like the purposeful shuffling of feet. Big feet. Sophie, becoming less and less skittish the longer she was in this place, slowly opened her eyes. Standing over her was a tall man. The sun shone behind him making it hard to see his face but surrounding his mass of long dark ringlets in a halo.

"Oh, hi.", she said as she sat up in the swing, "You must be Maria's friend."

"I am.", he said smiling as he stepped into the sunlight and leaned against the rail, giving Sophie her first good look. He was a sight to behold. ...about her age, long and thin, but muscular, like a surfer. He wore red and white baggies but was otherwise naked. His dark brown curls hung past his broad tanned shoulders. He had high cheekbones and full, perfectly formed, red lips. She wondered for a moment how they tasted. Sweet and salty she imagined. She moved her focus to his eyes, they were the color of honey. He met her gaze with a gentle intensity that she found incredibly appealing. He smiled at her again. His eyes locked on hers without an ounce of shame. She looked away, which made him chuckle softly.

"I've been waiting for you, for a very long time.", he confessed.

Sophie smiled, as her doubting mind regained near complete control. She was no stranger to the attention of men. She had once been approached by a guy whose opening was, "I want you to bear my children." Another time, while sitting outside at The News Cafe on Ocean Drive, she noticed a man staring at her from behind the wheel of his car. He smiled and winked, paying more attention to her than the car in front of him, which he eventually rear ended. One suitor told her she had "well articulated knees". He later admitted that the comment was the most original sounding compliment he could come up with. He felt mentioning her eyes was too predictable. The list went on and on. She used to find the lines flattering, now she just thought them silly, bordering on the ridiculous. Anyway, the gorgeous creature standing before her did have a sincere delivery, but really? Sophie never understood what anyone found so interesting about her that they were willing to embarrass themselves for her attention. She knew she was attractive, based on the responses she got from men, but she never really saw it for herself.

"That was a bizarre line... Creepy even.", she replied.

"Creepy?", he laughed good naturedly,

She liked his laugh. "Very."

"...a creepy line...", he repeated shaking his head.

"Yes.", she said dryly. This was her version of flirting.

"What if I told you it wasn't a line, what if I explained it to you? Would you believe me then?"

She thought for a moment about all that had happened. Why did this meeting have to be ordinary when everything else here had been extraordinary? Anything had become a possibility, and honestly she didn't really care if he was telling the truth or not. This man needed no line nor explanation. He had captured her already. Something about him was so comfortable and familiar, like home.

"Actually, given recent events, I probably would. Anyway it would be nice to think someone like you has been waiting for me." The wind blew her dress up over her knees. She quickly moved her hand down to cover herself. The move elicited another quiet chuckle from him.

He paid the closest attention to every move she made, as if he were trying to memorize each detail of their meeting. She noticed his big beautiful hands and long fingers as he held the arm of the swing and lowered himself to sit next to her. His hands moved delicately but were supremely masculine at the same time. He is perfect, she thought, and he smells...exactly as he should. He smelled clean. Underneath the smell of soap and the ocean, was him, and he smelled better than both.

"That's good to know.", he said then looked at her sideways, as Maria had done earlier; he added a wicked little grin for effect. "Now that I know you'd believe me, I'm not gonna to tell you. What's the point?"

She widened her eyes and sat up straight on the swing, "What!", she said laughing in shock.

He flashed a smile at her again, then stood up from the swing and dove off the porch and into the ocean. She jumped up and looked over the railing, just as his head popped out of the water.

"Come in!", he shouted. "I'll teach you how to do something cool."

She looked down at the dress. "Wait! Let me change.", she shouted back.

"Nope, now or never."

"...but it's Maria's, I don't want to ruin it."

"Oh please...por favor..." he shouted back. "You won't, besides she has like a million of them." He paused, "...you know, you could just take it off." He smiled again and raised his eyebrows at her.

Sophie clucked her tongue at him. "Thanks, you're so helpful."

He feigned innocence and smiled at her, "Anytime."

Maria did say to do what feels natural....and for the life of her she couldn't think of anything that felt more natural than this.

Sophie climbed up onto the railing. He watched her with a happy fascination she had not noticed before. She was a vision in the white dress, which in contrast made her skin appear golden. Her long hair blew behind her in the wind. She made a "v" with her feet, placing her big toes together as she had been taught when she was a little girl. From her sides she drew her arms up over her ears, hands above her head with thumbs tucked under. She bounced up onto the balls of her feet, then in one flawless motion dove into the ocean without a splash to be seen.

He smiled a smile that reflected pride.

She surfaced just in front of him.

"Impressive.", he smiled.

She smiled back, then caught his eyes looking down into the water in front of her. She looked down at herself. "Why did I even bother with the dress?", she said as it became clear what had caught his attention.

"That's actually sexier..."

She rolled her eyes at him. "I thought you were going to teach me how to do something cool."

"Nah, I was just trying to get you in the water. I can't believe you fell for that actually."

"Ah!", she let out a little gasp then slapped the water sideways in front of him. He was fast and turned his head away before the splash.

She put out her arm to try again, but he caught her hand and pulled her over to him. They were face to face, bodies touching. He was so warm and strong; she felt safe in his arms. She looked deep into his eyes, there was a kindness there. She didn't understand why, but she trusted him, she who trusted no man. He kissed her and she kissed him back. His lips were so soft... She was right, sweet and salty.

"I really have been waiting for you...", he said, "...for a very long time. I knew you'd come here eventually."

Sophie listened intently as he continued. "I dreamt of you when I was twelve; I've been looking for you ever since. You know that."

Sophie looked at him quizzically, she did know that. "How do you know it's me?", she asked.

He smiled at her and moved the hair from in front of her left eye. "It's you. The first time I saw you, you were glowing. Do you remember that day at Bayfront Park?"

She started to shake her head no, then stopped. She did remember something, a feeling, him... Sophie looked up at him, studying every detail of his face. "I do remember...you were watching me.", she smiled. You kissed me after I put on that strawberry lip gloss...we danced and laughed...it was at a concert...a big one."

He smiled, "I'm so happy you carried that memory with you. I didn't think you would forget me completely. Anyway, that's why I'm here, to remind you. Nothing can keep us apart, I'll always come for you."

Sophie was comforted by his words and the familiar warmth of his embrace. He loved her, and she loved him. She couldn't remember all of the details just yet, but she was sure of that.

They held each other in the water for some time without speaking until Sophie looked up at him again. "Where are we?", she asked.

He pursed his lips and wrinkled his brow. "The where, isn't as important as the why. Mama, you have a lot of work to do here, a lot of old wounds to heal. There are parts of yourself that you've shut down; you need to open them back up. Do you remember why you came here?"

"I don't remember much of anything. I just sort of woke up and was on the beach alone."

"You're not alone. I'm here, and I'm not the only one."

He pulled her closer. She wished she could climb inside of him. "Come with me.", he said as he released her. They swam next to each other over to the ladder. He held his hand out for her to go first. She climbed up onto the porch, and found two of Maria's white fluffy towels waiting for them on the swing. He was already behind her.

"Who left these here?", she asked.

"Does it matter? I'm just glad they're here."

She had to agree. He removed his red and white baggies and wrung them out over the railing like it was the most natural thing in the world to do. ...to stand there in the sunlight, completely naked in front of her absolutely devoid of shame. She admired him. He turned to pick up a towel and caught Sophie staring at him in awe. He wrapped the towel around his waist and tucked the corner over the top. His smile was disarming. "Are you just going to stand there in that wet dress? You'll drip all over the house."

She smiled, it was her turn, she wished she'd changed before he was finished. Now he had nothing else to do but watch her. She lifted the sheer dress over her head, stepped out of her panties and wrapped her hips in a towel. She walked to the railing and gently wrung them out.

He traced the tan lines on her back with his finger. "I have always loved these.", he said. She smiled, she knew that too.

"I need to rinse the dress out in fresh water and hang it to dry." She carried the garments into the shower of the guest room. He followed her. She hung the towel from around her waist on the hook and turned on the water. She rinsed the dress out in the cool fresh water then hung it over the surrounding wall to dry. She turned toward him as she began to rinse her hair. He stood there, still wrapped in his towel, watching her. "I miss seeing you like this", he sighed. She smiled at him as she held her arms up to finish rinsing the salt water from her hair. She turned and held the cobalt blue bottle out to him. He let his towel drop to the floor and joined her in the shower. She stepped to the side as he took the bottle and began to rinse his own beautiful body in the clear water. He opened the bottle and squeezed a few drops of the oil into his hand. It wasn't the lavender oil she had been expecting, but gardenia instead. She turned her back to him so he could rub the oil into her skin. He obliged. She turned to face him. He continued the task with total devotion. He massaged the oil into every part of her body. When he was done, he placed the bottle back on the shelf and turned off the water.

"You said I had work to do here. Where am I supposed to begin?"

"You've already begun by grounding yourself.", he continued, "Why don't we move on to releasing some shame?", he asked.

"What?", that was not what she had been expecting to hear. He smiled lovingly. "Shame. You've been carrying it with you for too long. It's blocking you from moving forward."

He was right. She lived in a state of shame for too long to remember, she was ashamed of her thoughts, desires, her body... Had it always been that way? She couldn't remember. Sometimes she would overcompensate by behaving shamelessly, in order to disguise her self disgust, though it only made her feel worse about herself afterwards.

He leaned forward to kiss her. She welcomed his lips. He took the towels and arranged them on the floor, then reached up for Sophie's hand and helped her down onto the towels. Her upper body was on the towels in the guest room while her lower body stretched into the shower. He kissed her again, everywhere. She looked down to see his big hands on her stomach, they were so tan against her skin. He looked up at her and smiled while kissing her slowly, repeatedly.

"Relax, ok?"

She nodded in agreement.

She quieted her mind and relaxed her body as he began to massage her from the inside out. He pushed down lightly with his other hand on her belly. She sat up immediately feeling a familiar pressure inside of her. "Stop! You're going to make me wet myself." He did not stop, "Shhh, you won't.", he laughed. She was in ecstasy, and both of them knew she didn't wan't him to stop, as she made no real attempt to stop him, but still she continued to warn him about what she felt was imminent. "Please...it's so embarrassing...please...stop..." He recognized her shame talking.

He tried to reassure her but she continued telling him to stop, convinced that some unfortunate accident was about to take place. He switched tacks. "So then pee."

"What?!", she said in shock.

"Go ahead, I want you to." She knew that if she let go, she would.

Sophie laughed, "No!"

"Trust me, you won't, and if you do, so what? You're in the shower.", he said. She laughed again and decided to throw caution to the wind. So what was right.

She felt something happening inside of her, something she hadn't felt before, a fullness. She tried to force whatever it was out by bearing down, but it didn't work. Exhausted she leaned back and just released, everything. She thought about shame and how useless it is. So what if she peed and he saw? Everyone does it, why should she feel ashamed about such a common activity? She felt tears well up in the outer corners of her eyes and softly roll down her face. What is going on?, she wondered. ...then came the flood. She had no idea she had been carrying all of that water around with her. She was amazed and laughed with her love, who was beyond pleased with both of them.

"I told you, you weren't going to pee."

Sophie felt the most relaxed she had ever felt. It was as though a huge invisible weight had been lifted from her. She swore she could actually see better, all of her senses were heightened. She was infinitely calm, happy, in touch with herself and with him. She sat up and kissed him. He climbed on top of her.

"I don't remember your name." said Sophie.

He smiled, "Amado."

Amado, she thought to herself. She was from Miami, she should know this. Spanish...amor, love...amar, to love, was all she could figure. Amado?

"What does it mean?", she asked.

"Beloved.", was his response.

Chapter Five : The Light Bearer

Sophie walked into the living room wearing a calf length, red, sleeveless, cotton jersey dress. The neckline scooped down low in a "u" shape, as it did in the back. It was cut on the bias and accentuated every delicate curve of her body. Simple, comfortable and elegant, Sophie loved it. Maria laid out the dress for her along with a variety of scented oils, toiletries and hair accessories. What she had done to deserve such kindness, she had no idea, but she was grateful to be receiving the bounty Maria was giving.

Amado stood in the doorway of the house watching her as she rearranged her hair.

"Do you like it?", Sophie asked, lifting the sides of the dress.

"Very much.", he said admiringly.

He wore a loose white t-shirt and matching linen draw string pants. He looked to her like a bronze god.

"Come here...", he said holding out his hand, "...I want to talk to you."

He led her over to the very same spot on the floor where Maria had calmed her the night before. Still basking in the afterglow, she couldn't imagine ever needing to be calmed down again.

"We're going to the party, if you still want to go, but we won't be traveling together.."

Sophie was not pleased by this information.

"I want you to close your eyes and breathe."

She hesitated, but did as he asked. "Now, focus on the indigo light just between your eyebrows. Do you see it?"

She nodded gently.

"Good. Stay there for a minute, don't try to hold on to anything that pops into your head, just let the thoughts pass through. Now, visualize a place, the first place that comes to mind."

She saw a beautiful forest and a cave carved out of the side of a large hill.

"You need to go and handle some old business in that cave before we can meet at the party."

A thought flitted across her mind, "How does he know what I'm seeing?", but she didn't hold on to the thought. She let it float by.

"If you don't come to me after a time, I will find you. I always find you."

She winced slightly.

"Are you afraid?"

She nodded with her eyes still closed, loosely holding on to the image of the cave.

"Don't ever let fear stop you from doing something you want to do. You want to go, don't you?"

She nodded.

"Good. You've already begun the journey baby. You can do this. Expand on your vision, relax into it, get lost in every detail of it."

His voice became softer and softer...

"I will come for you."

...until she couldn't hear him at all.

****

When she opened her eyes she was alone, standing at the entrance to the cave. She was still in the red dress, barefoot and smelling of gardenias, but she was older, by about five years. She sniffed the salt air and knew she wasn't far from the beach. Why had she come here? The earth was damp beneath her feet and the bed of dying leaves that carpeted the ground stuck to her soles. It was unpleasant, she hated the feel of it.

Sophie walked forward toward the cave slowly, with trepidation. The closer she got to the mouth of the cave the stronger the subtle feeling of dread she had learned to live with, grew in her belly. Her guts were constricted with fear. As she stepped into the cave she saw a yellow glow coming from somewhere deep within the cavern. The smell of cedar and sandalwood filled her nostrils, the incense calmed her, and kept her moving forward.

From behind an outcropping of rock, a woman appeared. She was tall, taller than Sophie even, and stunning.

"So you've finally come.", said the woman in a beautiful slow Southern drawl. It was Sophie's favorite accent. It reminded her of her grandmother.

"I have.", said Sophie.

The woman waved her hand and a sea of yellow candles perched in every nook and cranny of the stone cave blazed to life. Sophie was taken aback by the ease with which the woman accomplished the highly improbable. The woman's hair was long and golden blonde, like an angel in a renaissance painting. Her skin was creamy white, and her eyes were a soft shade of gray. She smiled at Sophie. Sophie did not return the smile, her instincts told her this woman was not to be trusted.

The woman bent slightly and a massive red velvet and mahogany throne appeared behind her. She sat, legs crossed, in the chair with her long delicate hands gently grasping the two perfectly carved balls at end of each of the chair's arms.

"*I* am curious by nature...", began the woman, "...please indulge me a few questions."

Sophie nodded in agreement.

"Darlin' you used to be fierce. I loved watching you. Nothing stood in your way...child, *you* had a fire in your belly. Then bit by bit they beat you down, stole your fire and worst of all, you let them. You've become just so...submissive; it's sad, pathetic even..."

Sophie, unfortunately, did not disagree. This wasn't the first time she'd heard the sentiment. Odd she thought that both times it came from the lips of a Southerner. Her grandmother's delivery was different, "What in the hell has happened to you? You didn't used to be afraid of nuthin'.", was exactly what she had said. True or not, she was unamused by the woman's insults.

"I thought you said you had some questions.", Sophie responded with her left eyebrow lifted almost to her hairline.

The woman smiled slyly. "...so it's not completely gone I see. Well, *that's* good news I guess.", she paused to adjust the sleeve of her dress. "What I want to know is why you're here. Why now? I mean, you've had plenty of opportunities to set things right."

The woman flicked her left wrist in Sophie's direction. A humble looking chair appeared behind her. "Please...", said the woman, "...do sit."

Sophie sat down on the cane chair. "I'm not sure why now. My memory hasn't been right since I since I arrived."

"So you're here because *they* pushed you to come, not even knowing *what* you were facing? Hmmmmm...", the woman clicked her nails on the arm of the chair. "Maybe that's for the best." She continued, "...and when it was time for you to leave your warm and fuzzy place, this is where your minds eye brought you?"

My warm and fuzzy place, Sophie thought. She hadn't considered Maria's house to be her "warm and fuzzy place", but it did pretty well fit the description.

"Yes, this is the first place I saw."

"Well then...", said the woman as she stood, "...let's get on with it."

As she stood her mahogany throne disappeared, Sophie jumped up just in case.
"Good call.", said the woman as Sophie's chair vanished. "...for future reference, *always* stand for your Queen."

The woman sashayed toward the middle of the vast room. "Being the gracious creature that, I am, I've decided to help you out. Let's *jog* that memory of yours shall we?"

Before Sophie could respond she heard a soft rumbling coming from the earth in front of her. A tendril from some sort of plant pushed it's way up through the soil. Quickly it grew thicker and branched out. The branches sprouted buds which opened into leaves. When all was said and done a miniature tree stood between them. Sophie looked up at the woman who was smiling in front of her, clearly pleased with herself. "Pay attention.", said the woman, who then redirected her own gaze back down to the tree. Sophie followed her lead.

The leaves on the tree lit up and seemed to come to life. She looked closely at the leaves and saw that every leaf had a scene from her life playing on it in a continuous loop.

There she was as a skinny nine year old, in shorts, loading the dishwasher in the kitchen. She remembered what happened next. As if on cue, her first stepmother entered the kitchen and started poking her nine year old self in the thighs. "You see that? You see how that shakes? You're going to be fat, just like your mother." Her stepmother laughed and walked out of the kitchen. Then the loop started again.

There she was on another leaf as a sixteen year old. She was sitting on the floor and crying as she emptied her dresser drawers into giant black garbage bags while her mother screamed and beat on her locked bedroom door. "You're a whore! You spend more time on your back than you do standing up! I want you out!"

There she was at three years old, waiting on her grandmother's doorstep with a little suitcase in hand. Her grandmother opened the door and ushered her inside, looking out toward her mother's parked car.

On another leaf she was 24, trying to leave the house of her ex husband. He was lying on the floor holding onto her leg and crying. She dragged him forward with her as she made her way toward the door.

The next leaf showed her at twelve walking home from school. A group of girls walked up from behind her, "Hey Sophie, I'd like to meet your mom...all ten of them.", one of the girls called out. Blank frames ticked by, at first Sophie was confused, then she remembered she had blacked out while she was beating the girl. The next scene on the loop was Sophie being pulled off the bloody twelve year old.

She was 25 in her old apartment on Miami Beach. It was dark and she was on the phone. Her ex-husband's voice on the other end said, "If you don't come and get everything that reminds me of you out of this house, including him, I'm going to kill myself. I don't know what I might do with him." "Why did you take him then?! Don't do anything!", yelled Sophie, "I'm coming now!" The voice on the phone went dead, Sophie screamed, "Stop! NO! Please, I'm coming!" Silence. The voice returned, "Bang, bang baby, it's all over." The loop began again.

There she was at eight years old, naked and wet from the shower. She stood in front of a full length mirror on the back of her grandmothers bathroom door. She was quietly talking to her reflection. "You think you're so great don't you? You think you're pretty? Well you're not. You're nothing special at all!" Her grandmother's voice interrupted Sophie's bathing ritual, "Sophie baby, are you about done?" "Yes meemaw, I'm coming!"

On another she was 27, sitting at a conference table with a judge, her ex husband and his attorney. The judge spoke, "I hope you're not giving up because these two have bludgeoned you to death?" "Yes...", Sophie answered, "...I am. I feel like we're each holding one of his hands and pulling, they won't let go until they tear him in half. I'll be the one to let go." The judge shook his head as tears streamed down her face. Her ex and his attorney smiled at each other. The loop began again.

She was 30 on yet another leaf, sitting at her desk at their home in Naples. She was reading a note attached to a photograph she had requested of her son. He was twelve in the picture, holding a guitar. She looked at his image with love and pride. The note was an excerpt from an old Paul Simon song. "...Oh what a time, what a time it was, a time of innocence, a time of confidences. Long ago, it must be, I saw a photograph. Preserve your memories, they're all that's left you." The loop ended with Sophie hanging her head and crying.

On another leaf she was ten. She watched her second stepmother yell at her in front of packed but opened suitcases on the bed. Sophie remembered this, the woman had no intention of leaving. She just wanted to create a show for her father when he got home. Her father walked into the bedroom and saw the suitcases. Suddenly, she was in the maroon and white Oldsmobile with her father. He was yelling at her...

Sophie turned away from the tree and the torturous little excerpts of her life. There were hundreds more. She looked up at the woman with the familiar sadness in her eyes. The sadness she hated in her own reflection. The haughty woman had become solemn. "Ring a bell?", she asked.

Sophie wiped the tears from her eyes. "Several."

Sophie looked at the woman carefully.

"I know who you are.", said Sophie.

"No...", said the woman, "...you only *think* you do. You don't *truly* know me."

Sophie watched very carefully as the woman walked seductively around the cave.

"I don't want to *truly* know you."

The woman turned her beautiful visage toward Sophie.

"Well now, you've gone and hurt my feelings, haven't you?"

Sophie was speechless and quite shocked by the notion of her having feelings. The woman read her thoughts. "Of course I have feelings. I may not be human...in other words, I'm not a *slave* to them, but we are all made of the same basic elements." The blonde woman laughed. "The entire cosmos is made of the same basic elements." She stopped to regard Sophie, "You don't know *much* do you?"

Sophie knew enough to know she was in a very precarious position with a rather dangerous and temperamental entity.

"No...", said Sophie, "...I don't."

The creature seemed pleased with Sophie's response. Nodding her beautiful blonde head in agreement. "*I...*", continued the woman, "...am a force for good in the world."

Sophie laughed out loud at the idea.

The woman's gray eyes grew dark. She cocked her head to the side and spoke, "You doubt my veracity?"

Sophie immediately regretted laughing.

"Well...", began Sophie cautiously, "...I have always understood you to be pure evil."

The darkness lifted from the angel's eyes. She put her hands on her hips and grinned slyly, "*Darlin'*, we've already established that you don't know much...and *I* am not pure anything, but when did you hear me say I wasn't *evil?*"

"You said you were a force for good in the world, how is evil a force for good? It makes no sense."

Sophie suddenly remembered that nothing here had ever made any sense.

The woman held her right hand out, palm up. A vision of Sophie's ex husband appeared floating just above her palm. "Remember him?"

Just looking at him made her feel sick. She nodded her head, "That, is the most evil person I have ever known."

The woman laughed. "We *clearly* don't travel in the same circles...but, perhaps.", said the blonde demon dismissively. "*That*, my dear, is the man who taught you how to love. You owe him a debt of gratitude."

Sophie was shocked and horrified by the comment. She felt a violent anger born of hellish pain rise up from inside of her. "...taught me how to love?! Are you insane? Do you have any idea what he did to me?! ...to us?! He knew nothing about love, he was a monster!"

"Was he? Sugar, didn't anyone ever tell you there are no such things as monsters? There are only people...only energy..." The woman smiled and raised her eyebrows at Sophie. She was enjoying Sophie's hate and basking in its radiant glow.

"...and yes, I know what he did. I helped him. It was *my* hand that guided him."

Sophie's eyes grew wide, anger flowed from every pore of her body. "You *helped* him?!" Sophie flew at the woman in a violent rage. The woman raised her left hand and stopped Sophie in her tracks. Sophie was frozen in place.

"*Look at you!*", the evil woman laughed.

She walked around Sophie, inspecting her thoroughly, approvingly.

"How *dare* you?" she laughed admiringly, "...just how I like 'em...", she said to herself, "...pretty and stupid." She stood in front of Sophie and winked.

"You know, I *chose* this body for you. I thought you'd like it. Even the accent, I picked it out *just* for you. I thought it would remind you of home. You see, I am *not* unkind."

She put one hand on her hip and tapped the index finger of the other on her chin, "I wonder, how inclined you would have been to attack me if I had appeared to you in some *other* form." The woman paused, "You *know* what I mean don't you?" Sophie looked at her but was unable to nod her head. Again, the woman read her thoughts. "Don't worry sugar, it was rhetorical."

"We've *all* seen the paintings, honestly they're not very flattering and so damn *boring* already. I thought I'd give you something new.", she sighed. "Oh well, no matter. Your little outburst helps illustrate my point." She turned her back on Sophie and flicked her delicate left wrist in Sophie's direction. Sophie was released. She collapsed to her knees and gasped for air.

"...you see..." she continued, "...we *all* have lessons to learn, and some lessons are easier to learn than others. It is also true that *some* people are easier to teach than others." She lowered her head and looked up at Sophie accusingly. "We all have different methods of teaching." She waved her hand nonchalantly through the air. "*I* am of the opinion that the best way to teach a lesson, and really make it *stick* mind you, is through a shock to the system." With that she cracked a whip next to where Sophie was kneeling. Sophie jumped, she hadn't even seen her pick it up.

"You told me that you *knew* who I was, but you thought nothing of attacking me. Why?" She paused for a moment. "Because I appeared to you in this soft and appealing form. Would you have been so keen if I had appeared in any of my *other* bodies? ...I don't think so. Would you have learned to love so well, so completely and deeply had you not first experienced...*him*?" She smiled. "You left that relationship knowing exactly what love was *not*, which in turn opened your heart to exactly what love is. You were an idiot before then. You had *no* idea. Any *jackass* off the street could have told you they loved you and you would've believed them." The fearsome woman laughed. "Would you have fully appreciated *him*...", she held out her left hand and Amado appeared floating above it, "...if you hadn't first known *him*?" She held out her right hand and a projection of her ex husband appeared again.

She had made her point. "Probably not.", Sophie said.

Lucifer was pleased. She moved her hands to her hips and the images of the men disappeared. "If it makes you feel any better, he'll probably come back as a *cock-a-roach*."

"No...", said Sophie, "...it doesn't. I kept waiting for him to have some huge epiphany before he died, but it never happened. I feel sorry for him."

The woman smiled, "Don't bother honey, it's a waste of energy. Anyway, as I said, *everyone* has lessons to learn."

"What was his lesson?"

"*That*, I am not inclined to say.", she demurred.

Sophie considered Lucifer in all her glory, though she still didn't trust her, she saw that the creature wasn't entirely evil. Perhaps there was still a little angel left from before the fall. More than anything, it was the sheer power of her will that fascinated Sophie. She could bring anything into being just by willing it to be. Mind over matter thought Sophie.

Sophie returned her attention to the little tree that was still endlessly replaying the most painful and depressing moments of her life. She didn't need a visual. Those moments were alive and kicking inside her head unchanged for years. She heard the cacophony of hurtful words, sobbing and pain continue to echo in the cave, Sophie was finally done. "Enough!", shouted Sophia. Lucifer smiled and bent slightly at the knees summoning the mahogany throne once more. She sat and lifted her legs, a matching red velvet ottoman appeared. Sophia did not notice. The fear and pain she had been holding inside for so long had transformed into anger. She started to breathe in a powerful way. Inhaling forcefully and exhaling quickly, causing her diaphragm to jump up and down with an exaggerated motion. A barely perceptible smile crossed Lucifer's lips. Sophia was rekindling the fire in her belly. It grew hotter and stronger until her midsection and the space in front of it and behind it began to glow with a yellow light. Thin filaments of yellow light extended beyond her body from the ball of fire Sophia was creating within. The air crackled with heat all around her. Sophia opened her eyes very slightly, just enough to softly focus on the little tree before her. On an exhale Sophia directed all the filaments of yellow light at the tree. As was her intention, the tree burst into flames. Lucifer smiled. Sophia kept the heat directed at the tree, she forced all her hate and anger through the yellow threads of electricity. The flames grew, but the tree remained unchanged. Apparently all her hate and anger wasn't enough. The scenes kept playing on their never ending loops. Sophia released the tree from her will. The fire went out and the tree stood in place exactly as before.

Sophia remembered the old story of the sun and the wind, and the argument they had about which of the two was more powerful. She had been playing the role of the wind. Sophia looked up at Lucifer who had been enjoying the show. "*Well?*", she said. Sophia ignored her and refocused her energies. She stomped her feet on the ground repeatedly. This time Sophia imagined the veins and arteries in her body were roots. She imagined them growing out from the bottom of her feet into the earth like the roots of a tree. She pushed all of her hate and anger down through her roots and out into the earth. She was grounded. Getting rid of those heavy emotions cleared out so much space, she was able to pull energy up from the Earth through her roots. Sophia lifted her arms into the air and imagined they were branches. She received light from above, as a tree receives energy from the sun. She pictured each and every leaf on the little tree, growing from her branches, one at a time. She watched the scenes flicker across the leaves with detachment. Sophia imagined the seasons changing from summer to autumn. With the arrival of autumn, the leaves began to wither and die, falling from the tree one by one on their own, taking the painful vignettes with them. Autumn turned to winter, and Sophia imagined her branches completely bare. The weight of the snow was light compared to the heavy load she had been carrying. As spring arrived, beautiful new leaves began to sprout from her branches. She filled these leaves with love, kindness, and visions of happiness. She saw all three of her children laughing and smiling in the sun. She saw herself, healthy and glowing. She saw Amado smiling and holding her in his arms as they rocked on the porch swing. Leaf by leaf she built the life she wanted, the life she knew she had a right to, the life she deserved.

Sophia breathed in deeply. The scent of sandalwood and cedar lingered in the air. She brought her arms down and slowly opened her eyes. It was dark. The only light in the cave shone in from the opening through which Sophia had entered what seemed like a lifetime ago. Lucifer, her throne, and the candles were all gone. The only thing that remained was a perfectly normal looking little tree. Sophia knew it would die without the light of the sun and showed compassion.. She bent over, took it by the trunk and rocked slowly side to side until she was able to pull it loose from the earth with its' root system still intact.

She blinked her eyes, as she left the cave carrying the tree, adjusting to the light outside. A few feet in front of the cave was a patch of sunlight. Sophie carefully lay the little tree down on its' side. She picked up a rock and began digging a hole deep enough to accommodate the tree's roots.

When she was done planting the tree, she stood back and looked at her work. She was very pleased with all she had accomplished.

Chapter Six : Protective Custody

Sophia did exactly as Amado had instructed her before. This time when she opened her eyes it was late afternoon, nearing dusk. She had no idea what day it was, nor how much time passed since her visit with Lucifer, but she got the distinct impression that it had been a long while. Sophia was still wearing the red dress, but she filled it out differently. Her hips and breasts were curvier than before, she had gained a little weight making her appear less lithe and more womanly. She looked down at her feet which were dirty from walking in the woods. Dirty feet were something Sophia, who loved to walk barefoot, simply did not abide.

Sophia stood near the edge of the forest, she could hear the waves crashing on the beach. She breathed a sigh of relief, nothing was more comforting to her than the sound of the ocean. Even the sound of a rough ocean, like today. Sophia walked toward the water. She took off the red dress, spread it out on the sand and anchored it in place with a large piece of coral that had washed up on shore. She entered the ocean carefully and with respect, as one must when dealing with such a powerful force. Sophia bathed in the ocean, washing off all traces of her foray into the forest. She emerged from the ocean clean. She shook the sand from the dress and slipped it back over her head.

The wind was blowing hard from the south. If she listened closely she could hear what she thought were drums, and voices floating on the air, but who they were and what they were saying was overpowered by the tides of Mother Nature and the direction of the wind.

She looked down the beach. Where the forest met the sand, was a thatched hut. The hut itself looked like it had been recently built, as the palm fronds were still green. It glowed from the inside. "...from candle light.", Sophia assumed.

As she approached the hut it became clear that someone was playing the drums. ...an African beat, like the kind she knew from old Cuban songs about the saints. She heard singing in a language that was definitely not Spanish, and then she smelled deliciousness. It was all coming from the north side of the hut, which protected the revelers from the wind. As she rounded the corner, she heard the sound of Amado's laughter. He stood in front of a fire, laughing. She watched his long curls bounce with every movement he made. Gathered around the fire were Maria, a beautiful woman Sophia did not recognize, an old man, and a huge muscle bound black man who was playing the drums.

The woman Sophia did not recognize was dressed in a yellow skirt that hugged her hips and a golden bikini top. She danced seductively around the fire, stopping occasionally in front of the drummer who was completely mesmerized by her. In fact all the men were taken by her, and why wouldn't they be? She was the image of femininity and beauty. Sophia's gaze shifted to Amado, who was no longer laughing, just watching the siren dance. Why wasn't she jealous? Sophia thought to herself. She stood quietly watching the scene for some time wondering why she wasn't bothered. Isn't it natural for a person to see something beautiful and want it? Even in the most fleeting sense? The old man was the least interested in the dancer, but even he stopped talking to Maria occasionally to watch her with intent. She wondered how Amado would react if he knew she'd been watching him clearly desiring another woman. Maria was sitting by the fire, cooking. Every now and then she'd look up at the beautiful woman and smile warmly. She wasn't bothered by her either.

Eventually the drummer stopped playing and the dancer stopped dancing. Everyone broke out into cheers and laughter. The dancer kissed the drummer passionately which brought more cheers and applause. Sophia started toward the group.

Maria saw her first and came running toward her across the sand. She welcomed her as a mother welcomes her daughter home from a long absence. "You decided to come after all!" Sophia didn't count her arrival as a decision, but supposed Maria was right, it must have been. Sophia smiled and embraced Maria tightly. She had missed her. Maria kissed her on both cheeks and hugged her back ferociously. Over Maria's shoulder she saw Amado waiting for his turn.

"Chi Chi, you finally made it.", he said. "I thought I was going to have to come and find you again."

Maria released Sophia and turned to face Amado. Both women smiled adoringly at him. Sophia was so pleased that she hadn't forgotten them this time. Amado held his arms out for Sophia. She rushed into them. He picked her up and spun her around in the air. The smell of him was intoxicating, what was it about his skin that smelled so good to her? They kissed lovingly, without shame. Behind them the drums started up again as did the laughter. Amado put her down and took her hand as they walked toward the others. Maria had already returned to the fire where she and the beautiful dancer were lifting the lid of a large pot hanging over the fire. A wave of saffron, garlic and seafood floated past Sophia's nose.

"Oh my God, that smells amazing!", said Sophia to no one and everyone.

The women looked up from their pot and smiled appreciatively.

Maria called out to Sophia, "Mama, come meet my sister."

Sophia turned to Amado and kissed him on the cheek. "I'll be back.", she said.

"I know.", he smiled. As she turned to head over toward Maria, Amado gave her a quick swat on the behind. Sophia jumped, startled but not at all displeased. She winked at him and continued on her way. The old man, and the man playing the drums laughed and smiled, enjoying the interaction almost as much as she did.

"Sophia, this is my sister Caridad…"

"...what a beautiful name.", said Sophia sincerely. Caridad smiled, "Call me Cari". Cari leaned forward to exchange cheek kisses with Sophia. She smelled so good Sophia thought, like honey and cinnamon. Somewhere in the depths of her consciousness a memory stirred. Sophia leaned back and examined Cari closely. "Have we met?"

Cari looked at Maria knowingly. "Not recently, no.", Cari and Maria giggled like schoolgirls who shared a secret. "I see you both attended the same classes on evasive conversation." Maria and Cari, laughed even harder sucking Sophia in to their merriment. Sophia sat down in the sand next to them. She turned her gaze across the flames and watched Amado talking with the men. He sensed her eyes upon him and motioned for her to come over. Sophie carefully shook the sand off the red dress and walked over to him.

"Hello.", said Sophia to the men. They smiled, the old man held his hand out to shake hers. He clasped her hand in both of his at first, but then before speaking he removed the cigar from his mouth and offered, "I am Nino."

"Pleased to meet you Nino.", Sophia replied.

"Encantado.", said Nino.

Sophia had always loved that response, rarely did anyone say "enchanted" in English anymore, but in Spanish it was still fairly common.

"El placer es mio.", the pleasure is mine, Sophia answered.

Nino smiled a crooked smile and winked at her.

The big dark skinned man who was playing the bata` drum held his huge rough hand out to her. She took it; her hand looked tiny and pale white in comparison to his. He was strong but didn't feel the need to squeeze her hand aggressively the way some men do. Instead he treated her delicately. "Santo.", he said with a twinkle in his eye that reminded her so much of Amado. All three of them had a very similar look in their eye, but the old man's was slightly different, he was definitely the most mischievous of the three.

"Santo, nice to meet you.", she said. This made them all laugh. She knew why, she was certain she knew them too, but had somehow forgotten them, again. It was always the same, Why did she constantly seem to forget people from here? She just shrugged her shoulders and was about to respond to their laughter when Maria called, "It's ready...esta listo."

"Please, ", said Sophia, "Maria, let me serve, it's the least I can do."

Maria happily relinquished the serving spoon she had been holding. Sophia knelt in the sand between Maria and Cari. Cari removed the lid to the pot. The paella smelled incredible. Sophia took a wooden bowl and filled it first for Nino. Maria held out another dish filled with platanos maduros, sweet fried plantains. Sophia served Nino more than his fair share something told her he liked sweet things. She handed the bowl to him, again he winked at her in response. Next she served Maria, picking out a choice piece of lobster for her and extra shrimp. Maria smiled and kissed her forehead as she took the plate. Sophia picked up another bowl and served Cari. She turned toward Cari and held out her hand. Cari handed her what she had been expecting, a little jar of honey. Sophia let a little honey drip onto the plantains making them extra sweet. Cari smiled warmly, as Sophia laughed. "I honestly don't know how you eat them like that." Cari just shrugged, "It makes me sweeter amor."

Sophia reserved the largest bowl for Santo. He was clearly the biggest with the biggest appetite. She saw a habanero pepper on the plate with the plantains and placed it on top of his bowl of paella. He smiled appreciatively.

Lastly she served her love. She filled his bowl with a little bit of everything. Sophia stood and walked over to him. He kissed her before taking the bowl from her. Everyone looked to see that Nino was eating, he was, which meant they could all begin.

****

After the bowls were washed in the ocean, they all lounged around the fire, which Santo kept blazing. It wasn't cold out, but the warmth of the fire counteracted the slight chill of in the night air that was blowing with such energy. They passed around a bottle of aguardiente and the men smoked cigars. Maria spoke, "As we all know...well almost all of us...", she turned to Sophia, who was relaxed in the arms of Amado, and blew her a kiss, "...we are here to say goodbye to an old friend." Her words snapped Sophia to attention. She knew that she had been invited to a party, but didn't know it was a going away party. Everyone but Sophia nodded their heads. Maria stood up and held her hand out to Sophia. She turned to Amado, "Am I the one leaving?" "In a sense...yes.", said Amado. Sophia was hurt, she didn't want to go yet, and didn't understand why he was so nonchalant about her departure. ...he, who claimed, would always come for her. Amado and Maria had been so good to her. Maybe her streak of good luck with them had finally run out. In her heart of hearts, Sophia couldn't believe that. She decided to just continue to trust them and go with it. With some sadness and a nagging sense of betrayal, Sophia stood up and took Maria's hand.

Maria led her toward the hut and opened the door. There on a cot in the middle of the room lay a little girl sleeping. Sophia had been mistaken earlier. While there were some candles burning, the glow from inside the hut came from the girl. She'd never seen anything like it before. The girl was surrounded by a soft white light, like a giant halo encompassing her whole body.

The two women stood there in silence. Sophia watching the little girl sleep, and Maria watching Sophia. Something about this child was incredibly familiar. She wore a pair of old sneakers, a t-shirt and jeans. Her hair was a long brown mess sprawled out all over the pillow and obscuring her face. Sophia's attention returned to the jeans. They were an old style, from the seventies. LuvIt jeans, Sophia remembered. On the back pockets were quilted satin hearts in the colors of the rainbow. Sophia turned to Maria, and before she fully comprehended what the words meant, said, "I loved those jeans.". Maria's eyebrows knitted together and a sad smile crossed her lips. In that instant the realization of what was happening hit Sophia, she began to sob uncontrollably. She was looking at herself, exactly as she was on that night. The night when the pretending ended. The night she lost her father, and lost herself to the woods. Tears rolled down Sophia's face. She covered her mouth with her hands to keep from waking the child, but it was no use, she was stirring. Sophia bit her lip as the ten year old version of herself sat up in the bed. Sophie put her hand to her head, the child was in pain. She was still bleeding from the wound she received that night running through the woods. Maria walked over to her bedside and sat on a stool next to the bed. She wrung out the cloth that was floating in a basin on the the makeshift nightstand next to the bed, and patted Sophie's wound with it delicately. Sophie was clearly familiar with this routine. She smiled appreciatively at Maria and hugged her around the neck when she was done. Maria looked up at Sophia, Sophie's eyes followed Maria's until Sophie and Sophia were caught in each others gaze. Sophie smiled reassuringly. "It's just me. I've been waiting for you.", said the little girl.

"I'm so sorry.", Sophia replied sniffling and fighting back the tears as she sat down next to the child on the bed. Sophie climbed into Sophia's lap. They embraced each other tightly.

"I didn't know how to get to you. I didn't know...I didn't know you were still here...or that you were still in so much pain. I thought I was supposed to forget and move on... I'm so sorry I left you in the woods that night...so, so sorry.", Sophia said between the tears.

"It's ok.", said Sophie. "They've been taking care of me."

Sophia turned toward Maria.

"How long has it been?", Sophia asked Maria.

"Thirty years.", said Maria softly. Sophia continued to cry, mourning the loss of time. Time spent apart from one of the purest aspects of herself.

Sophie released Sophia from her tight embrace so she could look her in the eyes. Sophia moved the hair back from the child's forehead, the wound was gone. Sophia kissed the spot where it was, then met Sophie's gaze again.

"You left me here to protect me. ...to keep me safe. This is where I needed to be until now. It's safe for me to come out now."

Maria smiled and said to Sophia, "This is not a place you can get to just because you feel like it. You have to be ready to come here Sophia...there are certain locks in place that keep you from getting here before you're ready. You could not have done it before. You are here now, because it was time. That's all."

The door to the hut opened and one by one Nino, Santo, Cari and Amado filed in. Sophia was not only surprised that they all fit in the tiny hut, but that the hut seemed to grow in order to accommodate them. Cari came over and hugged Sophie affectionately. "I love you mamita. Look how your ya ya has healed." She kissed the girl on the head. Next came Santo. He picked her up and squeezed her. She looked like a rag doll in his massive arms. "You know how to call me if you need me, right?" Sophie nodded and kissed him on the cheek. "I'm always here.", he said pointing at her heart. "I know." She hugged him tightly around the neck before he put her down.

Nino sat down on the stool where Maria had been sitting, and waved Sophie over to him. She followed happily. He beckoned her to come closer so he could whisper something in her ear. Sophie and Sophia laughed out loud at the same time, no translation needed. Mischievous he is, thought Sophia. Sophie gave the old man a kiss and a hug. The little girl looked up at Maria who was smiling through her tears

The old man shooed the others out of the way, clearing the path to Maria. "You've been like a daughter to me, all these years... I will always be with you. You know that don't you?" Sophie nodded her head and kissed Maria's hands. The hands that had taken care of her for so long. Sophie looked up at Amado. "Thank you Amado. Thank you so much for helping us get here. She needed you, your love, to do this." Amado smiled at Sophie, "I'll see you soon, we'll all be together again soon."

Sophie climbed back into Sophia's open arms. Their embrace was so tight and so complete that they merged back into the one that they were. Sophia just sat there, absorbing the moment, when she felt the familiar tugging sensation near her navel.

Chapter Seven : I See, Said the Blind Man

Sophia stood at the foot of the most magnificent art nouveau bridge she had ever seen. The steps leading up to the bridge were huge rounded slabs of white marble. Anchoring the steps on either side were massive pillars carved with lotus blossoms; the pillars were completely entwined in their roots. Atop each of the columns was an intricately carved statue of the dog Cerberus.

Sophia thought the placement of the dogs odd, as their bodies and two of their three heads faced the bridge, while one of the heads on each statue looked back over its' shoulder. It seemed more natural to her that the statues' bodies would face the foot of the bridge, as Cerberus was essentially a guard dog. Maybe they aren't guarding the bridge, Sophia thought to herself.

More peculiar than the orientation of the dogs was the bridge itself. Sophia turned and looked behind her. There was the green hut, just as she had left it, only now, leading from the door of the hut was a path that ran directly up to the bridge. When did all of this appear? She was certain both the bridge and pathway were new, as she surely would have noticed them last time she was here. It had been mere weeks, not months nor years, since her last visit.

She looked up at the dogs again, then behind her. "Maybe they're guarding the hut.", she said out loud. She liked that idea.

Sophia had grown stronger now that she was whole; since she carried the contents of the little hut with her, she saw no reason to go back. She decided instead to move forward and explore the length of the span in front of her.

She lifted the hem of her white gauze sun dress and took the first step.

She walked up the initial incline, which took no time as the bridge was low to the water. Once she reached the apex, the bridge leveled out before her. She peered over the edge and saw beneath the sun flecked surface of the turquoise ocean, a beautiful coral reef, teeming with life. Brightly colored fish, every shade of the rainbow, darted in and out of little hiding places among the nooks and crannies of the coral. Sophia smiled, it was a beautiful sight, she thought, as she continued along happily.

The bridge really was a sight to behold. The white marble rails were supported by delicately carved marble Calla Lilies, whose stems were arched in a semi circle. Every two feet or so the white marble was broken up by the blue ocean, visible through the hollow semi circle of the Cala Lilies.

After about an hour of steady walking, she began to question her decision. The breeze had gone and the heat reflected brutally up off the white surface of the bridge. How long was this bridge anyway? ...and where did it lead? She had no water with her and the humidity in the air was making it increasingly more and more difficult to breathe.

Sophia was extremely uncomfortable. She turned and looked back, the green hut was nowhere in sight. She leaned against the lily balustrade, and tried to catch her breath. Sophia was relatively fit, walking for an hour would have been nothing, under normal circumstances. However, the circumstances here were far from normal, she reminded herself. It felt as though someone was squeezing her neck, gradually increasing pressure with each step she took. She knew in her heart of hearts that she needed to continue forward, and willed her body to do so.

She pushed herself off the low wall and resumed walking, slowly, keeping near the railing for support should she need it, and after another fifteen minutes, she did. Sophia held onto the rail and looked down into the water again as she tried to catch her breath. The bright blue water was no longer bright blue. It was as though all the blue had been sucked out of the ocean. Everything suddenly appeared as though it was tinted red. Sophia looked up at the sky. It too was devoid of it's characteristic hue. She looked down at her hands; she was seeing the world through a red filter. Sophia thought perhaps lack of oxygen to the brain was to blame for the missing blue. She should have known better.

After a short but hard fought internal debate, she decided she had to turn around. She didn't think she would make it across the seemingly unending bridge.

As she turned her back on the way ahead, she felt something. The stone beneath her feet vibrated gently. Then came the sound of a rhythmic thudding...

Sophia looked up and saw an old man galloping toward her. He was running wildly, from side to side with very little direction. He appeared to have only the most general idea of forward. He bounced between the railings like a pinball. Sophia shouted "Stop!" as loudly as she could, to no avail. The old man continued barreling toward her. She waved her hands in the air desperately, but he did not see her. Sophia sprung into action with the little energy she had left. She tried to avoid the man by jumping to the side, but the old man suddenly changed directions just as she did and plowed directly into her at full speed.

Sophia first felt the impact of the old man's body slamming into hers, then the impact of her back and head hitting the floor. The old man was on top of her, now flailing wildly. She pushed him off of her with all her might. In one quick motion the old man flipped over onto his knees, and then slowly began to calm down, as he did this the realization of what had just happened, what he had done, started to sink in.

Sophia winced as she touched the back of her head. A large lump had formed instantly. She recognized the thick sticky wetness too. "Lord help me...", she said to herself. "...I walk in the world of the perpetual head wound." She sighed, then turned her ire on the man.

"You could have killed us both you know!" She shouted, but it came out as a raspy whisper.

The old man ignored her. He was still on all fours, collecting himself.

"I'm talking to you! Look at me!", Sophia paused to catch her breath, "What the hell is wrong with you?"

The old man began to carefully crawl toward Sophia. She instinctively pulled back. The old man held out his left hand and lifted his head. Instantly, she realized he was blind, and softened her stance. "...are you ok?", asked Sophia. The old man didn't answer, her words had no impact on him at all. He continued moving toward her with his hand extended. Sophia understood what the old man was doing. She took his hand and put it on her face. The old man smiled and sat down on the pavement next to her. Sophia saw that he was bleeding too, from his forehead. "Usted está bien?", Sophia tried again in Spanish. No response. The old man felt the features of her visage. Sophia watched as a flash of recognition crossed his face. She looked at him closely, and suddenly she knew him too.

The old man was deaf, dumb and blind. He never meant to hurt her, he simply had no idea what he was doing. He didn't hear her, he didn't see her, and he couldn't communicate with her. He was just running blindly from his own demons, and she was in his path.

Now that she understood, she was no longer angry. This wasn't about her, it was about him. Sophia began to cry. The old man felt her tears begin to flow. He held her face in his hands and kissed her softly on her brow. Sophia hugged him around the neck gently, then she took a deep breath and released him. The old man pushed himself up and continued on his way as if nothing had ever happened, stumbling and bumping into the rails as he went. She knew she couldn't help him, he would misunderstand her efforts. Ultimately, he was on his own path. Much to her surprise, she was neither sad that he didn't stay, nor happy to see him go. She was finally detached.

Sophia felt the back of her head tingle. She touched her wound then looked down to examine her fingers. The blood was gone. She was healed. Sophia sat there with her back leaning against the low wall of the bridge for some time.

She rested her hands on her lap and tried to focus on her breathing. A bumblebee flew past and landed on the rail next to her. Too exhausted to worry about a bee sting, Sophia continued to breathe as she watched the bee. She began to imitate the sound the bee made with her breath. She found it calming. Each breath gave her strength to overcome the self doubt she was experiencing regarding her decision to walk the bridge. She would forge onward after all. Besides, the red tint seemed to be less intense than it was earlier and her breathing was almost back to normal.

Sophia stood up and continued moving forward into the unknown.

Chapter Eight : Provenance

Sophia continued along the bridge. The heat had eased a bit as the breeze picked up slightly, but it was still sweltering. She was convinced that if only the blue would return to her world everything would be better.

She wondered where Amado, Maria and the others were. She kept expecting them to pop up and save her from the heat and complete exhaustion. So far though, they were noticeably absent.

Sophia walked slowly along. Her breathing was still labored, but it was a bit easier since her encounter with the old man. She let her hand drag along the marble railing. Her fingers slid over the carvings etched into the marble. Sophia looked down at her hand to see the design she'd been touching absentmindedly. There, under her fingers was a man carved into the stone. She stopped to better see the details of the carving. The man wore a horned crown, and stared straight forward as a tiger chewed on his leg. She wondered what it meant. As she leaned over the balustrade to get a better look at the side of the carving, she noticed a ladder leading down to the ocean. She looked up and down the side of the bridge, this was the only ladder she could see.

The bridge was just about twenty feet above the waves. She desperately wanted to go down the ladder for a swim; maybe she would find Maria again. She imagined the cool water and how good it would make her feel, how it always made her feel, but she was afraid to make the descent. She wasn't sure if it was fear of the ocean's unnaturally red color or something else. Sophia respected the ocean, but rarely feared it, especially when it was calm like it was today...something was wrong. She decided to keep walking.

She got about another twenty feet along when she stopped dead in her tracks. "Sophia..." Someone was calling her name. She saw no one in front of her, nor behind her. "It's the heat.", she thought to herself. "My mind is playing tricks on me." She began walking again. "Sophia." This time she was certain of what she heard. She didn't recognize the voice, it was muffled, like it was coming from under the water. With trepidation, she walked over to the side of the bridge, and looked down. Oddly, there was another ladder. She thought of the carving of the man. "Fearlessness.", she whispered. Sophia had been told by both Maria and Amado that if she was drawn to this place then she was here for a reason. "Might as well get it over with.", Sophia said out loud to herself.

Sophia stripped naked, and climbed over the side of the bridge and onto the ladder. She was breathing heavily, tired, and not operating at full capacity. She had no desire to become wrapped up in her ankle length dress and drown. She made her way carefully and deliberately down the ladder.

The ocean was warm, like bathwater. Sophia delicately lowered herself into the womb of all creation. "Sophia..." There it was again. The gurgling of the voice was unnerving. Something brushed past her leg. She was terrified, but she stayed put, treading water and waiting for whatever was going to happen to happen. Just then, a barracuda surfaced in front of her. Sophia watched in amazement as it began to speak.

"This is how you see me.", said the fish.

Sophia stuttered, "I..I..don't know what you mean."

"Yes you do."

The barracuda submerged itself. Sophia saw a silver flash under the water, then cried out in pain. The creature bit her on her left hand. Sophia watched in horror as the already red water became crimson with her blood. The cold scaly creature released her and resurfaced in the same spot where it had previously appeared. Sophia held her hand tightly to her chest, applying pressure in an attempt to stem the flow. This will bring the sharks, Sophia thought to herself in resignation, it always does. She'd been here before. Wounded, she was easy prey for the wicked and opportunistic.

"Why will you never forgive me?", the fish began to cry salty tears.

Sophia was stunned. "You just attacked me! You brought the sharks to me...how am I supposed to fight them off with one hand?!" With every word she spoke Sophia found it easier to breathe.

"Yet all I had to do to get you to come to me was to call out you..." Sophia could not argue with the truth. "If I'm so terrible, then why did you come?", asked the fish.

Sophia's nightmares were realized. In the distance she saw the sharks swimming toward her.

Sophia looked at the barracuda bobbing pitifully up and down in the water. Such a vicious creature, ugly and spiteful, yet still, it suffered. Alligators cry while they eat you. Sophia reminded herself. Sophia tried desperately to work out the barracuda's motivations as the sharks drew closer, but it was no use. How could she ever understand the machinations of a cold blooded fish?

Sophia began to pray. "Maria, please help me. I don't know what to do, I'm stuck mama, I need you."

The fish sneered at her, "She's not your mother."

"She is my mother, and yours!"

"Then where is she?" The barracuda swam closer to Sophia...to comfort her. "I'm here."

Sophia recoiled from the the fish's advance. She swam toward the ladder without turning her back on the barracuda.

The smell of coconut oil wafted past Sophia's nose. Maria's voice floated by on the same breeze. "She's not really a barracuda is she? Release her."

Sophia looked closely at the fish. The fish's cold beady eyes began to soften and turn green. Its' pointed face flattened and jagged teeth receded and squared. Its' silvery scales faded and turned to pink flesh. Ultimately Sophia was face to face with a woman that looked remarkably like an older version of herself.

"Perception is reality.", Maria's voice whispered to her on the wind.

The woman was nervous...afraid, like an animal backed into a corner, unable to recognize friend from foe, and ready to attack again. She was much less dangerous in this form. Now she tried to hurt Sophia with her bark instead of her bite. It didn't matter anymore though, Sophia realized that the woman could not harm her, unless she allowed it, unless she accepted the woman's invitation to pain.

Sophia looked beyond the woman searching for the telltale fins. The sharks had disappeared.

"I can't do this with you anymore, I won't." said Sophia to the woman. "I will be there if you truly need me, because that is who I am...but I am done with the rest of this. It's not healthy.", Sophia said without blame or judgment, then began her ascension to the bridge.

The woman cried and screamed. She slapped the water and shouted insults at Sophia for leaving her down there. Sophia had no desire to hurt the woman, neither with words nor with deeds. She realized that in removing herself from the source of her pain, she may have made the woman unhappy, but that was not her goal. Sophia was done with repressing and denying her emotions in order not to hurt the woman's feelings. She climbed up the ladder to the bridge, found her dress right where she had left it, and calmly slipped it over her head. Sophia could still hear the woman shouting from below, but she knew the woman was fine. She was just being who she was.

Sophia sat down and rested. She wasn't sure if the woman had stopped screaming or if she had just stopped listening, either way, she heard nothing more. Happily, her hand was no longer bleeding and the bite marks were healing up, as she knew they would.

Sophia closed her eyes and allowed her mind to drift. Her thoughts took her to Maria and the hut. Since her reunion with Sophie, she found access to so many new memories. Actually, she wasn't sure if they were memories or dreams. Sophia banished the thought after a moments deliberation. She had become increasingly convinced they were one and the same.

Chapter Nine : The Gift of Maya

Sophie sat on the edge of the little bed in the green hut. Maria wrung out a clean cloth in the basin next to the bed.

"Come here mamita, let me clean that for you."

Sophie scooted over on the bed toward Maria.

"Ouch.", said the little girl softly.

"I know, I know, but if we don't keep it clean your wound will become infected.", she said as she gently pressed the cloth into the girl's forehead. "An infection here, will spread to the rest of you...the healthy parts of you.", she paused to wet the cloth and wring it out again. "I can't change what happened mamita, or heal you really...you have to heal yourself...but I can help make sure it doesn't get worse. If you let me."

Maria's words made sense to Sophie, so she sat still for her. She watched Maria's lovely brown hands move delicately but with purpose from the bowl to her head and back again. When Maria was finished she stood. Sophie looked up at her with eyes the color of the clearest ocean waters.

"Why are you being so nice to me?", asked Sophie.

Maria smiled. "Because you are my daughter."

Sophie looked confused. Maria smiled and sat next to her on the bed.

"You love the ocean don't you Sophie?"

Sophie smiled broadly, "I do."

"Why?"

"Why?", Sophie laughed as if this was the dumbest question in the world.

"Because the ocean is wild and beautiful. Because no one can control it. Because it changes all the time and it's filled with beautiful fish and plants." Sophie became more and more animated as she continued. She seemed to forget all about her head. Maria observed the child's gesticulations with a smile and a twinkle in her eye.

"I feel free when I'm in the ocean. Sometimes, I pretend I'm a mermaid." Sophie calmed down and turned to Maria in seriousness, "I'm a very good swimmer you know, I can even swim with my legs together like a mermaid would."

Maria couldn't help but laugh. Sophie's eyes grew wide, "It's true! I really can!"

Maria nodded her head. "I know mama, I've seen you do it."

Sophie was puzzled, "You have? When?"

"A million times.", smiled Maria. "I'm always with you Sophie, but you notice me most in the water." Sophie's eyes narrowed. "I've never met you before...I mean, until I came here."

"Yes you have, you just don't remember."

Sophie shook her head no. "I would remember you, for sure."

Maria returned Sophie's narrow eyed look, playing with the child.

"Do you remember that time when you were seven...you were playing mermaid by yourself in the water off Haulover Beach...and your grandma was laying down on the towel? She had just closed her eyes for a minute..."

Sophie's eyes widened as the memory came to her. "Yes! The day I got sucked under. Oh, that was so scary."

"You were never caught in an undertow before, were you?"

"Nope."

"Did anyone ever tell you what you were supposed to do if it happened?"

Sophie looked up at the ceiling thinking back, "No."

"Do you know how people drown most often in an undertow?"

Sophie shook her head no.

"They panic. They try to fight the ocean...", they both chuckled at the idea of fighting the ocean, Sophie even rolled her eyes at the thought which Maria found completely adorable, "...they gasp for air where there is none and swallow water instead. Why didn't any of that happen to you? How did you know to stay calm and just hold your breath until the undertow released you?"

"I don't know. I just did."

"I was there with you Sophie."

"I didn't see you."

"No, but I was there."

Sophie knit her eyebrows together and looked Maria over. Maria laughed, "Let's go swimming."

"Ok. That still doesn't explain how I'm your daughter."

Maria laughed, "No, it doesn't, does it?"

Sophie shook her head no.

Maria shrugged her shoulders. "A mother just knows these things."

Sophie rolled her eyes again. Maria held her hand out to the girl and pulled her up from the bed. Sophie winced, on standing.

"The salt water will help heal you."

Nino was apparently standing just outside the door, as he opened it for them. Sophie smiled at the old man. Nino winked at her from under his straw hat and handed her a coconut. He had cut the top off the coconut with two strokes of the machete.

"Toma", he said, as he offered her the coconut.

Sophie looked at Maria. "He wants you to drink it.", Maria said.

Sophie took the coconut from Nino, "Gracias", she said.

The old man laughed again and walked away. Sophie tipped the coconut up and took a big sip of coconut water. It splashed on her face and ran down onto her shirt.

Maria smiled, "Don't worry, it get's easier."

As they walked hand in hand down to the beach Sophie heard the sound of metal clinking and tinkling. Off to her left Sophie saw a little girl, about her age, dressed in a beautiful purple sari, with golden bangles on each wrist, she was kneeling in the sand under a palm tree. Sophie looked up at Maria for permission to go to the girl. Maria smiled and nodded her head yes. "I'll meet you in the water when you're done.", said Maria.

"Ok.", said Sophie as she walked toward the girl.

"Hi.", said Sophie as she approached the Indian girl.

The girl looked up and smiled. "Hello.", came the response. Sophie was fascinated by the girl's accent, she had such a lovely lilt to her voice.

"Do you mind if I sit with you?", asked Sophie.

"No...", said the Indian girl, "...certainly not."

The girl extended her open hand and gestured to a spot on the sand next to her. Sophie sat down. "My name is Soph..."

"Sophie, I know.", said the little girl smiling. Sophie didn't like being interrupted by a girl of her own age, and the fact that the girl knew her name made her immediately suspicious. Sophie glared at the girl through slitted eyes. The girl found it amusing and laughed sweetly.

"My name is Maya, I have brought you a gift."

Sophie softened her eyes but still regarded Maya distrustfully. Maya reached down into a fold of fabric and pulled something out. Sophie watched carefully, but could not see what the girl held in her fist.

"Hold out your hand," directed Maya. Sophie's curiosity got the best of her; she held out her hand. Maya smiled and opened her fist less than an inch above Sophie's outstretched palm. When Sophie felt the hard and smooth object hit her hand she closed her palm and brought it closer to her face so she could inspect the gift more closely.

"It's a prism.", said Maya.

"Thank you," Sophie said to Maya, "but why are you giving me this?"

"As a reminder." Maya said matter of factly.

"A reminder of what?"

Maya paused for a moment, then gently took the prism from Sophie's hand. "Look at the light from the sun shining between the leaves, what color is it?"

Sophie turned her face up to the sun. "White.", she said, blinking repeatedly.

"Is it?, asked Maya who immediately held up the prism causing the white light to break apart into red, orange, yellow, green, blue and violet rays of light.

"Hmmmmm.", was all Sophie had to say.

Maya smiled at Sophie. "Did you know," Maya continued, "that if you catch the light just so...", she twisted and turned the prism slowly until the light hit one of the surfaces at a very sharp angle and lit up the whole shape, "...you can create something called total internal reflection?"

"No, I didn't.", said Sophie. "Cool."

Maya smiled, "Indeed. Very cool. It happens when the prism reflects ALL the light, rather than just breaking it apart into different wavelengths. You can use the prism as a mirror, see?" Maya moved her head to the side in a motion Sophie understood to mean move in closer. Sophie scooted over next to Maya and saw herself in the mirror of the prism. She was a mess, her hair was wild, matted, and blood was still oozing from the ugly, bruised gash on her forehead. Though Maya was seated right next to her, her image was not reflected in the prism. Sophie turned to Maya quickly to reassure herself that she was still there. She was.

Maya smiled, "Sophie, this gift is a reminder to you that what we see is not necessarily what it appears. Sometimes it is necessary to construct realities in order to veil ourselves from knowing things before we are ready to know them, to protect ourselves. Are the many colors we see actually one, or is the one many? Are there any colors at all, or are they just a reflection of you, of what you have created? You will have to answer these questions on your own, but until then, keep this prism with you so that you will not get lost in whatever reality you choose to build for yourself in the mean time. There is often great difficulty in finding the way back to who we are from who we have become. When you are ready, look to this prism and remember you can only truly see yourself when you are illuminated from within, and you can only really know yourself through total internal reflection."

Sophie took in everything Maya had said for a minute. Maya handed the prism back to Sophie, who gripped it firmly in her hand.

Sophie looked closely at Maya, examining every detail of her face, then asked, "How old are you really?"

Both Maya and Sophie laughed, which caused Sophie obvious pain.

"I am ageless and timeless Sophie. I am merely an illusion."

Chapter Ten : Actualization

Sophia opened her eyes and found she was still sitting on the bridge. She smiled and stretched her arms out above her head as though she was just awakening. She brought her arms down and ran her fingers through her hair, shaking it out in the back, and combing through the tangles with her fingers. As her fingers slid down her head, they came to rest on a rope tied around her neck. It was slimy, as though it had been soaking in the fetid water below for a very long time.

Sophia was surprised, she wondered how long the rope had been there. Her fingers worked furiously to untie the slippery knot, and when they did the rope fell onto her lap, to her horror it was pulsating. She figured it would be tinted green from algae, but with the red filter, it was a sickening pinkish color. Sophia stood up, allowing the rope to fall from her lap to the floor. She inhaled sharply and let out a powerful yell.

She screamed so loudly her whole world shook causing the bridge to buckle and waves to rise up in the sea. Even the fabric of the heavens seemed to be moved, and billowed with the force of her scream. Brilliant blue light shot out from her mouth and filled the ocean and sky with the color they had been missing.

Upon completion of her violent exhale Sophia was calm, and as the calm returned to Sophia, so the calm returned to the world.

She was finally free, unblocked, and the energy within her flowed completely unfettered. No one could stop her, but herself. (The commonly proffered concept when actually realized is beyond potent.) It had always been that way, she just didn't know it, until now.

She smiled. "I am thirsty." As soon as she spoke the words a golden cup adorned with pomegranates appeared before her on the balustrade. She reached for it and took a sip. Sweet tea. She smiled again, and began naming what she wanted. "Amado.", she said aloud. A second cup appeared before her, as did Amado. She was delighted. He smiled at her approvingly and nodded for her to continue. Amado drank from the cup as Sophia continued. "Maria, Cari, Santo, Nino!", one by one they all appeared before her, smiling the same approving smile as Amado. Sophia stopped for a moment and wondered if her next thought was possible...of course it was...everything was she concluded. "Meemaw." Sophia opened her eyes and watched her grandmother emerge from her own chest and land on the bridge directly in front of her. She looked exactly the same as the last time Sophia saw her, blonde bob and all. Sophia was overcome. She began to cry tears of joy, sadness, and pain all of which intermingled. As in life, her grandmother could only tolerate tears for so long.

"All right, all right. Now that's enough."

Sophia smiled and embraced her. Her grandmother smoothed her hair and kissed her on the head.

"I have missed you so much.", said Sophia.

"Baby, I've been with you all along. You know that. Don't you?"

Sophia nodded her head, "I do, but I wanted this." Sophia gestured to her grandmother's form.

"All you had to do was say so."

Sophia smiled.

"Hey", said her grandmother, "I'm proud 'a what you've done. You let it go...like water off a ducks back. You're acting like *my* baby again, the child that *I* raised." Her grandmother winked at her. "Don't you know you can do anything you want? You just have to do it. Nobody can stop my baby." Her grandmother reiterated what she already knew. Sophia took it as permission to keep going, to keep exploring possibilities. "Thanks Meemaw, I love you so much."

"I know you do baby, I love you too."

"I can see you like this whenever I want?"

"Whenever you want."

Sophia smiled and opened her arms wide. Her grandmother smiled a proud smile back at her and jumped back into Sophia's heart, where she had always lived.

Sophia looked at the group and raised her eyebrows. She could tell by the expressions on their faces that none of this was new to them. So rather than explain anything, she blew them a kiss then leapt off the side of the bridge and dove into the ocean. The sea was cool, clear and the most beautiful shade of blue Sophia could imagine. She swam past coral reefs and schools of fish faster than she had ever swam before. A group of dolphins joined her. They jumped in and out of the water around her laughing and smiling as they do, but struggling to keep up with her. *They* had to surface for air, Sophia didn't. She used to dream of being able to breathe under water. Now she was doing it. All the oranges, greens, blues, yellows and purples of the seascape appeared as blurred stripes on either side of her as she flew past. She turned and headed back toward the bridge at breakneck speed. When she had just about reached the bridge she shot straight up out of the water and hovered in front of her little family. Her hair and dress were completely dry and just kind of floating as if suspended in space around her. They laughed and clapped for her. "Sigue, sigue!", shouted Nino. Cari smiled, "Yes, keep going!"

Sophia crossed her legs underneath her body and floated down toward the surface of the ocean. Like a lotus flower, her roots stretched into the earth and up through the water, but she herself floated above the water without getting wet. She closed her eyes and with her mind's eye began to imagine a house.

Building materials flew across the water from points unknown as she constructed a home from her comfortable seated position. Piece by piece a house appeared to assemble itself in front of her. Though of course, the house wasn't assembling itself. Sophia was assembling it. She was both architect and carpenter.

Sophia had never really had a home, a place she couldn't be thrown out of on a whim nor have to run away from. There were places where people had allowed her to stay for a while...but never really a home. Now, however, it was her intention to create one. A place where her soul and her soul's mate could rest easily.

When she was done a modest but beautifully crafted cottage floated in front of her. She opened her eyes and smiled. It was perfect, exactly as she imagined it, built of stone and wood with an arched entryway and copper screen door adorned with dragonflies and waterlilies. The front door was wide open and inviting. A broad front porch stretched across the full length of the house, and was punctuated on one side by a trellis covered with passion vines, and on the other by a bent wood porch swing. She softly waved her hand to the left in front of her. The gentle motion caused the house to rotate in that direction. Sophia wanted to examine her work from all sides. She was pleased. The smell of dinner and freshly baked bread wafted out of the open windows of the house. She filled her home with the energies of love, joy and kindness, loyalty, and passion.

Sophia looked up at Amado. He was watching her still, from the bridge.

"I love you.", she spoke to him without saying the words.

He smiled. "I love you too", he said aloud.

"This is our home.", she said to him again in silence.

"I know.", he answered silently. He crossed his hands over his heart then released them quickly. A metallic green butterfly fluttered out from underneath his hands and landed, perched, on her outstretched finger. Sophia motioned toward the cottage with her finger. The butterfly took her directive and flew over to the porch swing.

It occurred to Sophia that some of the people she loved and respected most in the world were standing around on a hot bridge watching her. She wasn't quite ready to come up yet; she knew there was still more to be done. So she decided to provide for them what they could certainly have provided for themselves. She figured if she could build a house out of nothing more than intention, there was no limit to what they could do. Still, she knew they liked it when she did things for them, a small sacrifice, an offering of a little something to thank them and let them know she was thinking of them, honoring them.

Sophia closed all but one of her eyes again, and willed an image into being. Within a few moments she heard laughter, cheering, and the playing of drums. Sophie smiled. She opened her eyes and looked up at Amado. He was blowing her kisses. Maria walked over to the railing and laughed.

"Do what you have to do amor. We're here for you. Como siempre."

"Like always!", repeated Amado.

"Oye!", Maria regarded Amado, one Cuban to another, with mock seriousness. "She understands me, ok?!"

Sophia laughed. She always found joy in their interactions. "I may be gone for a while, I don't know how long this will take.", Sophia said.

"Mama, have you forgotten already? Time doesn't matter, come when you're ready. You know how to find us. ...eng we no how to fine ju.", was Maria's reply. She rolled her eyes at Amado. Amado laughed as Maria took him by the arm and led him away from the railing and over to the party.

Sophia knew how blessed she was.

She stood up over the water and allowed herself to float above the bridge. From this vantage she could see they were at its' midway point. She looked down. Santo was playing his bata drums, Cari was dancing in front of him. Maria and Amado were standing to the side laughing and joking with each other. Maria waved her hand to get Cari and

Santo's attention, then pointed up at Sophia. They all waved and exchanged goodbyes. Nino sat by himself at a table set for five, eating a piece of coconut flan, his dessert before his dinner, like a child. Sophia was happy to see the old man eat. "Nino!", she called down from above. He looked up from his flan. "Keep me on the right path." Nino nodded his head and winked at her. He took off his straw hat and waved it with a flourish.

Sophia peered down the remaining span of the bridge. It seemed so silly to walk the rest of the way when she knew she could fly.

Chapter Eleven : 9 / Completion

The miserably hot afternoon had turned into a beautiful, breezy and cool late afternoon. Sophia flew toward the end of the bridge. She didn't flap her arms like a bird, she simply moved forward through space at a rate of speed she desired. Her hair blew in the wind behind her. Her dress did the same and tickled her ankles in the process. She loved the feeling of the cool air passing through her toes she thought as she wiggled them.

A thought occurred to her. She was using flying as a means to an end, to reach her destination quickly. She slowed down and allowed herself some time to play. She leaned backward turning backflips in the air. All the while giggling happily, like a little girl. Then she reversed the motion and turned somersaults in the air. She dove down and flew just above the surface of the water, skimming it with her fingertips. She bent her torso up slightly and ascended rapidly, she put her arms up over her head and spun around like a ballerina. Her dress floated out around her body as she turned. When she finally stopped, she drew her legs and crossed them under her and just looked around. She was astonished by the sheer beauty of the world as seen from above.

She turned her attention to the bridge, whose path she was following. In the distance she saw two giant columns flanking the bridge exactly as she had seen at the entrance. The columns themselves were the same, engraved with beautiful lotus flowers, but Cerberus had been replaced by what appeared to be eggs. She couldn't tell for sure, but they did have the familiar oval shape. Sophia squinted, the eggs had something wound around them. She grew impatient with her limited vision. She wanted to be there now so she could see, and then she was.

She floated cross legged, near one of the sculptures, indeed, it was an egg, a very large egg; she could easily have fit inside. Each was wrapped by a serpent. Orphic eggs, Sophia remembered.

She turned around, still hovering, and surveyed the beach in front of her. It was identical to the one at the other end of the bridge. The only noticeable difference was the absence of the green hut and walkway.

Just as she planted her feet in the warm sand, she noticed a flickering light appear amongst the trees. Sophia stood there in the sand waiting and watching, no longer afraid of what nor whom would come. Finally a bent old hermit emerged carrying a small lantern. His hair was long and knotted into dreadlocks.

"Welcome!", he said as he made his way toward her.

She smiled warmly at him. "Thank you."

"You've come a long way.", said the old man. "I know it hasn't been easy, but you've done it!", he exclaimed. "You've broken the psychic ties that bound you to your past and kept you from realizing your full potential!"

She found his level of excitement charming, and contagious. She could feel her feet start to vibrate prematurely. The hermit noticed and smiled.

"Now that all *that's* been sorted out, you must be ready to complete this part of the journey, aren't you?"

Sophia nodded, "I am."

"Do you know what to do?", asked the old man politely.

"Yes, I think so.", she replied.

The hermit lifted the hem of his long claret colored robe and carefully stepped backward, giving Sophia the space she needed to grow.

Sophia took several deep breaths, then began to chant, "Lam." She gave equal focus to every sound that made up the word, allowing each tone to vibrate within her. She continued to chant the word lam as a soft red glow grew steadily from the base of her spine. "Lam", she chanted again and again until the soft red glow became two spinning vortices, in front and back of her.

Next she began chanting, "Vam" until a similar orange light appeared just above her pubic bone. She continued on with "Ram" and it's corresponding yellow light emanating from above her navel, "Yam" which produced a green light in the area of her heart, "Ham" a blue light at her throat, and finally "Om" which created an indigo light at her brow.

Sophia stood there lit up like a rainbow colored Christmas tree. Six of her chakras were open. The vortices spun in different directions, alternating from clockwise to counter clockwise.

Her body was literally humming with energy.

The old man smiled, and set his lantern down. The little illumination it provided became unnecessary given the festival of lights on display in front of him.

Sophia had achieved a level of concentration where her chakras would remain open and fully functioning without her undivided attention. She shifted her focus to the sleeping red serpent she imagined to be coiled around the base of her spine. She summoned it to awaken from it's lengthy slumber. The snake obliged and shot up her spine with the force of a tightly coiled spring and punctured something deep inside her head.

Eyes still closed, she dropped to her knees, then lowered herself onto her heels. She felt some pain as her skull began to open. She breathed through it and the pain was bearable. Slowly, the bone began to separate into in six pieces forming a triangular pattern. Gradually it unfolded and took the shape of a crown.

The process was somewhat obscured by the light Sophia emanated, but the hermit knew what was happening to his initiate. He smiled and shielded his eyes as Sophia's head began to sparkle. The change from bone to precious metal and stone had taken place. The area around Sophia was suddenly bathed in a soft white light shining down from above. The hermit admired her beautiful platinum and amethyst crown, then closed his eyes quickly as he knew what his initiate would experience next. A pillar of pure white light shot down from the heavens and entered Sophia through the open crown on her head.

Sophia breathed deeply and exhaled slowly several times. Though her eyes remained closed, she saw the crown on her head collapse back down onto itself. Effectively sealing her head shut and locking the pure white light within. As her head knitted itself closed, the light from above receded back into the sky. Leaving behind an undulating green and blue aurora.

One by one, she gently closed her chakras, like the petals of a flower closing up for the night. When she was done switching off all the lights, she opened her eyes. Sophia looked at the hermit and smiled. A chair appeared next to him on the sand. "Thank you.", he said and sat down. She remained there, kneeling in the sand, just being in the moment, as Maya's gift of illusion was obliterated.

Maria was right, of course, that Sophia had chosen to be here. She had. Not only had she chosen the place, but she had chosen the time, the circumstances and the players. Sophia understood all of this now. The fear, doubt, insecurity, anxiety and self loathing were all gone. Actually, she thought to herself. They never really existed until she created them.

Sophia looked at the hermit. "I had a thought...", she said, then paused for a moment, "...or did the thought have me?"

"Indeed.", replied the hermit.

She stood up and turned toward the woods. There watching from the distance were Maria, Cari, Santo, Nino and even Lucifer. Sophia could now see them for who the really were; four saints and a fallen angel whose name used to simply mean bringer of light, all brought here by her to help her on the road to realization. Sophia smiled warmly as one by one they dematerialized and rose up into the beautiful aurora over head.

Sophia closed her eyes and turned them upward to look at the space between the two lobes of her brain, "Om ma ni pad me hum.", over and over until the beautiful platinum and amethyst crown appeared on her head again. Now that she had already opened her seventh chakra it was easier, and much less painful to access at will.

The hermit walked over to her and extended his hand. She took it.

"Are you ready to go home?", he asked.

Again she replied, "I am."

Chapter Twelve : Beatitude

Sophia stepped out of the woods wearing a purple t-shirt, sneakers and a pair of old jeans. Her long hair hung loose around her shoulders and was streaked with silver. Evening was quickly approaching, but for now there was still a little daylight left. She looked across the dirt road and saw the house she built. Amado was on the porch swing with their daughter, while their sixteen year old son worked under the hood of his car.

Amado spotted her and waved. She smiled and waved back as she crossed over the dirt road and onto the lawn. Their son poked his head out from under the hood.

"Hey mom."

"Hey baby." she replied. He walked out from in front of the car. He was already as tall as his father, and looked just like him, but with her coloring. He leaned down and kissed her on the head, then bent down a bit so she reach to kiss him on his head. It was their custom.

He wiggled his dirty fingers in front of her and lifted his eyebrows in a a mischievous manner. She laughed as he pretended to chase her, and she pretended to run away. She made it to the porch as he disappeared back under the hood.

"Hi mama.", said their daughter as she leapt up from the swing nearly spilling Amado's drink. "Careful, careful...", he demanded. Both women smiled at him.

"Hi beautiful." she said as they embraced. This baby was olive skinned like her father, but with green eyes and Sophia's hair.

The fourteen year old released her mother abruptly as a car pulled into the driveway. "They're here!", she announced as she bounded off the porch and across the lawn to meet them.

Amado stood and opened his arms widely. Sophia looked up at him and smiled as she snuggled into him. Her shoulder fit perfectly into his armpit. He wrapped his right arm around her as they settled back into the swing. He handed her his glass. She took a sip...sweet tea.

"How was your walk?", he asked.

"Great.", she answered, grinning from ear to ear.

"Good baby, I'm glad.", he said as he squeezed her.

They turned their attention back to the lawn. Her eldest and his girlfriend emerged from the car. "Look at him.", Sophia said to Amado. "He's a man already."

Amado laughed, "That he is."

Their daughter hugged the girl, as their eldest made his way over to the sixteen year old and his car.

The girls climbed the steps of the porch.

"Mmmmm...smells good.", said the pretty blonde girlfriend.

"Thank you sweetheart. Go on in." said Sophia as she and Amado stood to usher the young women into the house.

"Boys!", Amado called out. "Dinner time."

Their sons put down the tools and walked up the front steps.

Amado's clone ran by them. "Wash!", shouted Amado while shaking his head. "...with SOAP!", he added.

"Smart.", said Sophia approvingly.

Their oldest came up the steps smiling.

He was lovely, thought Sophia. He had the most beautiful honey colored eyes that reflected the depth of his soul. Currently, they were sparkling. Good she thought, he's happy.

"Hi mom, hi Dad."

"Hi baby.", said Sophia. She hugged and kissed him on the neck.

He turned to Amado, and they embraced warmly. Amado kissed him on the head.

The young man smiled. "Well, what'd you make? It smells awesome."

"Your favorite.", answered Sophia.

"Sweet!"

Amado laughed and followed the boy inside. "No, no, no...you too.", he called after him. "I saw you with your hands under that hunk of junk. Wash!"

"Hey! I heard that, she's not a hunk of junk. ...che's got a few jears on her but che's a cream puff!", the proud owner shouted from the bathroom.

Sophia listened as laughter broke out in various locations from within the house.

"Ok, Mr. Montana, take it easy.", said Amado.

Sophia looked out across the dirt road and into the woods. It had taken some time, but she finally found her way home.

The End

My darling children,

DRV, AAC, and SMC

You are three unique, interesting and kind individuals. My love for you knows no bounds. Take care of each other.

ABC, I love you, now and forever.

Find me, you know I have no sense of direction, I'll be waiting for you.

Miss Eduff, I miss you every single day. So grateful to have known you at all.

Reviews

"The Red Speck" blends lush, sensuous imagery with raw emotion on an individual's otherworldly journey to psychological wholeness. Sophie's heartbreak leads her to awaken in an unknown but strangely familiar world in which she meets and learns from gorgeous archetypal characters tinged with the colors of Miami and the old South.
While an engaging story on its own, the reader will find genuine insight into their own fixations that hold them back from happiness, including hints on how to move forward. The author has a gift for taking airy spiritual and psychological experiences and thoroughly grounding them in the body. She accomplishes this by painting vivid, emotionally engaging scenes with words, evoking a visceral and sympathetic response in the reader in a manner similar to the techniques found in the poetry of Rumi. In this way the protagonist's alchemical transmutation of leaden emotions to joyous golden freedom becomes our own. Highly recommended." **Amazon Reader Review**

"I was immediately drawn in to the complexities of Sophia's life, presented in the form of an adult fairy tale. The psychological and philosophical difficulties and resolutions of everyday life were intelligently and enchantingly addressed. I felt as if I was with Sophia on her journey as image after image was presented to me and for me this is a priceless criterion." **Susan Scott, author "In Praise of Lilith, Eve & the Serpent in the Garden of Eden"**

"The writing...is beautifully ethereal and soothing. I have a deep fear of the ocean, but the excellently and appropriately titled The Red Speck made me want to plunge in. The book takes you on your own plunge into an ocean of discovery...I highly recommend The Red Speck and look forward to more writing from the author." **Lesley Abravanel Andersson, writer and columnist for The Miami Herald**

"I was profoundly moved by Siddhartha in my College years; this book has done the same for me in my forties." **Amazon Reader Review**

Made in the USA
Charleston, SC
17 January 2016